UNDRESSED TO KILL

"Strip," Byers ordered.

I thought about a whole lot of responses I could have made . . . if only this or if only that. There weren't any "if only's" I could appeal to at the moment. I stripped.

The uncomfortable truth is that a naked man *feels* totally vulnerable. Psychologically that is an immensely powerful reduction of the spirit. I hoped Georgie and Tim did not happen to know that.

"Get back in," Byers said.

I made no attempt to cover myself or to ask if I could at least retain my Jockey shorts. I didn't want to give the bastards that much satisfaction. I just got back into the cab. The vinyl part of the seat cover was unpleasantly hot against my thighs. At least there was fabric beneath my even more tender bare butt. Small favors and all that.

"Home, James," I said.

"Gee, it's gonna be fun killing you," Byers said with a grin.

A HELLER NOVEL

THE TURN-OUT MAN

Frank Roderus

BANTAM BOOKS

TORONTO · NEW YORK · LONDON · SYDNEY · AUCKLAND

THE TURN-OUT MAN
A Bantam Book / February 1985

ISBN 0-553-24595-3

Published simultaneously in the United States and Canada

Bantam Books are published by Bantam Books, Inc. Its trademark,
consisting of the words "Bantam Books" and the portrayal of a rooster,
is Registered in U.S. Patent and Trademark Office and in other
countries. Marca Registrada. Bantam Books, Inc., 666 Fifth Avenue,
New York, New York 10103.

PRINTED IN THE UNITED STATES OF AMERICA

H   0 9 8 7 6 5 4 3 2 1

For Gary McCarthy

THE
TURN-OUT
MAN

1

The car was definitely enough to attract attention. There aren't so many that fight the gravel road out this far to begin with, and most of those are hunters, rock hounds, or flatlanders trying to find a spot off the beaten path. Certainly few enough that the passage of a vehicle of any sort is enough to draw an inquiring look. And then you can almost count on its being a Jeep or a pickup truck or some damn-fool tourist in a motor home.

This thing was as out-of-place as a pimple on a Madonna's nose, and it brought my head around and my eyebrows up when I glanced out the living-room window. When it turned into my driveway, it brought me to my feet and heading for the door.

The beast was some kind of customized limo, no less, with a sure-enough landau—or would they call it town car—top. A Caddie, I saw, when the snout of the thing was aimed my way, and it had a ducky little open-air section for the chauffeur and a long, flop-top section behind for the gentry to ride in, behind their own separate windscreen. At this time of year, coming on spring but still on the chill side even in midday, the convertible top was up and so were the windows. The glasswork was heavily tinted, so I couldn't see what kind of royalty had come a-calling. Or more likely

1

had gotten themselves so confused that their chauffeur was going to have to ask directions of the local peasantry.

I opened the door with a sigh. Giving directions to the lost is usually a summer pastime. It looked like the season was getting off to an early start this year. I let the storm door slap closed behind me, put on a look of good cheer, and went out to do my duty.

The chauffeur, or rather the driver, of this landlocked gunboat was almost as much of a surprise as his vehicle. The man who stepped out once the thing crunched to a halt was not exactly my idea of anyone's hired hey-boy.

He was tall, quite a few inches beyond my five-eleven-and-a-bit, and heavily built without looking the least bit fat. The pinstripe suit he was wearing had not come off anybody's shelf—every line and hem broke at precisely the correct place—and his shoes had that gleaming perfection that can only be put there by someone who makes his living with Kiwi polish and loud popping cloth. The guy iced it when he advanced—that is the only way to really describe it, to simply say "walked" just would not do—through the muddy slop of the spring melt without looking down to see what he was stepping in.

"Mr. Heller?"

That *really* blew me away. I was prepared to give directions to a lost soul, not to be asked for by name by a man who looked like he would be on familiar terms with half the board members of the Fortune 500.

"Mr. Carl Heller?"

"Reckon I am." I will admit that something about the man, or maybe just the anomaly of the situation, made me drawl that out in as countrified a tone as I could muster. If

I'd had a hay stem handy I'd have stuck it in the corner of my mouth, too.

"Good." Any satisfaction he might have felt about being right was only in the choice of word. Nothing showed in his eyes or on his face to indicate approval or otherwise. "May I have a word with you in private?"

Some of the surprise was beginning to wear off. "This place is about as private as you can get unless you want me to saddle a couple horses and take you into the back country."

He looked around before he asked, "Are you alone here?"

"Until you drove up I was."

"Good." Again that flat, quickly spoken word with no tone or expression to flavor it.

Like I said, the surprise was about worn off. So was the novelty by now. Whoever this guy was and whatever he might want, he was about to piss me off. I'm kinda choosy about whom I welcome into the nesting territory, and this man hadn't yet said or done anything to make me think we had a budding friendship going here.

"Do you remember a man named Claude Bint, Mr. Heller?"

"Do you know that I can't think of a single reason why I should be answering your questions instead of drinking coffee and reading a good book?"

For the first time he showed some expression. A hint of a smile made his jowls spread a little wider. "Good." This time he sounded like he meant it.

The truth was that I remembered Bint quite well. I had performed certain services for the gentleman about two years ago, extricated him from an extremely unpleasant

4 FRANK RODERUS

situation, pocketed a sizable thank-you, and went my own way. The situation had been unpleasant enough to make me remember it for quite some time to come.

Which is the way I pick up a little extra pocket change from time to time. If anyone asks, I am just a high-country rancher running registered Longhorns and a few registered AQHA mares on a ranch near Lake George, Colorado. But the way I do it, the old-fashioned way of turning the livestock loose on undergrazed land so they can work for me instead of my having to work day and night for them, they bring in just about enough income to pay the taxes on the land. For those little extras like motorcycles and gasoline . . . and food . . . I need something more.

And a long time ago I discovered that the law is an interesting enough concept, but it has nothing to do with justice. Which I much prefer.

So from time to time I do favors for people who are entitled to justice but can't get it from the law. I'm not too proud to accept a gift of appreciation, preferably folding and green. I don't have any particular fee schedule, can't have because I'm not licensed to do anything, but it usually works out just fine for all concerned.

Claude Bint had thought so too. Or had the last time I saw him, which was right at two years ago now. The man had been halfway toward becoming a hood at the time. Maybe he had changed his mind since then?

I looked at this big, expensively dressed man in my muddy yard and decided very quickly that whoever and whatever he was, he was no hired gun sent by a belatedly irate Bint. Even if Bint had decided I had shucked him—and hell, he had decided how very much he appreciated my help when he had sat down to write out the check—I couldn't see any reason for that kind of reaction so long after the fact.

No, whatever this guy wanted it had little or nothing to do with Bint's long-forgotten problem. I eyeballed the fellow and waited for him to state his business or go away. Either one would have been just fine. I was not particularly hurting for money at the moment and really could not have cared less which he decided to do.

The man smiled and stepped forward with his hand extended. "I seem to have started off on the wrong foot with you, Mr. Heller. My apologies."

I got the impression that his apologies were neither given often nor offered with a whole hell of a lot of sincerity. On the other hand, he had made the gesture. I shook with him.

"I am Al Falcone, Mr. Heller. You can call me Al." He acted like I ought to know the name and be suitably impressed. I'd never heard of Al Falcone. "Could I come inside for a few minutes, Carl?" For the first time he looked down toward the muck we were standing in and made a face. The expression looked almost comical on that over-sized, impeccably groomed mug.

"Sure."

I led the way and as usual kicked off my boots at the door so I wouldn't track in mud. I managed to keep a straight face when Al Falcone bent to local custom and removed his soiled but still gleaming pumps by my door. It was decidedly strange to see him pad in silk socks across to an easy chair and settle into it. I had never had a visitor remotely like this guy.

"Claude recommended you to me, Carl," Falcone said before I could offer him a drink. "He suggested I verify that by mentioning the word *percolator*. I have no idea what that might mean, nor do I have any need to, of course."

I nodded. Falcone would not know, but Bint and I did. The papers, bond certificates actually, that Bint had been flimflammed out of that time had been hidden in a percolator in the con artist's apartment. That wasn't the sort of information that Bint would allow to become public knowledge, and I damn sure hadn't told anyone about it.

"I take it you have a similar problem, Al?" It seemed a safe enough conclusion at this point. Falcone looked like a businessman who might well deal in large sums. Large money usually means large risks, and sometimes there are those who like to nibble at the icing on other people's cakes.

"Since I don't know the exact nature of Claude's difficulties, Carl, I cannot comment on similarities, although I would tend to doubt there are any. Under the circumstances."

"What circumstances, Al?"

He looked at me without expression. "You should know to begin with, Carl, that I am the owner and operator of a respectable and perfectly legal brothel in the state of Nevada."

"You . . . ?"

"A whorehouse, Carl. I run a whorehouse."

That sense of surprise that had gone away? It was back.

2

"You disapprove," Falcone said calmly. I guess it wasn't hard, at that, to read my expression.

"Uh-huh."

"Is it prostitution itself that you don't approve of?"

I thought about that one for a moment. "No. That's the woman's choice. It's the pimps and scumbags who prey on them that I don't like."

Falcone's face became harder, if that was possible. "I don't have to justify myself to you, Mr. Heller." We had left the first-name chumminess, I noticed.

"I didn't ask you to justify anything," I reminded the man.

Falcone reddened slightly, then seemed to relax. "For a businessman, Mr. Heller, you have a decidedly independent attitude when talking with a prospective client."

"I'm a choosy son of a bitch," I agreed, "and no businessman at all. Ask around. I'm just a good ol' boy from the high country who raises a few cattle and a few horses."

Falcone cleared his throat. "So I've been told."

"Believe it," I advised him. "And you can leave anytime you like. It doesn't make a lick of difference to me."

The man gave me a cold look. But he didn't leave. I was

expecting him to. And wanted him to. I had less than no
desire to get mixed up in anything with a damned pimp and
his string of whores, legal or otherwise. People can choose
to do just about anything they want and I'll figure it's their
business and their privilege and leave them alone to do it.
But pimps and other such bloodsucking bastards piss me
off. Always have.

I should have known that this Al Falcone couldn't just let
it lie, though, especially after he had said he didn't have to
justify himself. Naturally, he turned right around and tried.

"Before I go, Mr. Heller, you should give me an
opportunity to explain the nature of the situation here."

I didn't say anything, but he went right ahead without
encouragement.

"First, in spite of what your impressions might be, I am a
businessman. A middleman, if you will. I operate fully
within the letter of the law, providing a clean, decent,
honestly operated place of business where the gentlemen
and the working girls can both satisfy their particular needs.
Comfort and gratification on the one hand, and a high level
of income on the other. I act," he smiled slightly before he
repeated the former secretary of state's peculiar phrase, "as
an honest broker in the matter. No more and no less.

"There are roughly a score of us in this particular, uh,
brokerage business in the state of Nevada. Ours is an equal-
opportunity field. There are women as well as men.
Orientals as well as Caucasians. The investors who provide
capital for the houses might well surprise you. They are
highly respected men and women who see an excellent
investment opportunity and reap the benefits from it."

The man was wrong there. Not that the money boys
behind some of the operations would be respected people; I

wouldn't quarrel with that. He was wrong that it would surprise me. It wouldn't. Not when there was a lot of money to be made. Plenty of people don't care where or how they make their bucks.

But I can't quite make myself forget that there is a helluva difference between the terms *respected* and *respectable.*

"Obviously you know rather little about the way legal brothels are operated in the state of Nevada," Falcone went on, and that one I couldn't argue with. I knew—and cared— just about nothing on that subject.

"Ours is a good business, Mr. Heller. And I am not speaking now about its income potential. I am speaking from the point of view of both client and employee. I have never heard of any customer being rolled in any Nevada brothel. He is free to negotiate an agreeable price for whatever service he wants performed and to walk away unmolested if an agreement cannot be reached.

"From the girls' point of view, they suffer no abuse in any of the legal houses. They are not beaten or mistreated in any way. They receive weekly health checks, and they operate without fear of arrest or shakedowns. They sign in for three-week periods of employment, and at the end of that time they are free to go anywhere they wish and do anything they wish without concern about health problems or arrest records.

"Obviously, the business itself is virtually as old as time. No society has ever succeeded in stopping it, and relatively few have tried. My colleagues and I are heavily taxed and provide social benefits to our communities at large. We are also quite proud of our record for honesty in our dealings with our clientele. And with the public in general. We make

it a point to act always with discretion and integrity. We
perform a public service, and we do it well."

It was all interesting enough, I suppose, but not particularly impressive. A man can take pride in just about
anything if he can find the right rationalizations for it.
Including, obviously, being a whoremaster.

"It all sounds like a world of pure sweetness and light," I
said, "so I kinda have to wonder what you're doing here." I
smiled. "Somehow I don't think business has gotten so bad
that you're out drumming up trade."

For the first time, Falcone looked uncomfortable. "I
. . . Claude suggested that . . ." He stopped.

I waited. If the guy wanted his hand held, he could go get
one of his tame hookers to do it for him. Giving comfort
was more in their line than mine.

Falcone cleared his throat and tried again. "Without
public support, Mr. Heller, or at least public disinterest, we
cannot continue to operate. The legalization of brothels is a
local option in Nevada counties, Mr. Heller. Any incidents
that would result in a public outcry could be . . . a
disaster for all of us."

Now, it seemed, we were going to get to the meat of it.
Threaten to derail a man's gravy train and you can expect
some howls in return.

Falcone cleared his throat again. "At the moment, Mr.
Heller, particularly with the NOW and certain others so
active, the political climate is such that we have to be
particularly careful of our public image."

"You're beating around the bush, Al," I prodded.

"Perhaps." He looked distinctly uncomfortable now.
"At the moment we have, uh, a potentially embarrassing
situation developing. Public disclosures would be awkward,

to say the least. And I, we, are assured that you are reliable and discreet. I am prepared, Mr. Heller, representing myself and certain other brothel owners, to offer you a 'gift'—our investigations indicate that you accept gifts rather than fees or commissions—a gift of fifty thousand dollars plus expenses if you agree to help us eliminate this problem."

I looked at the man and couldn't help laughing. "For cryin' out loud, Al, I don't know much about Vegas and the crowd that runs there, but from what I've heard, you didn't have to come all this way to buy yourself a hit man. And your information is a little off on that point anyway. That's not the business I'm in." I got up, fully intending to show the SOB to the door.

Falcone looked startled. "That is not . . . not at all what I had in mind, Carl. Not at all. Please understand that. We have to be . . . very cautious, very clean. We, all of us, are under constant suspicion. From the police, from the public, from the IRS, everyone. That is not at all what I meant to imply."

"What do you mean, Al?"

"There is a man, a newcomer to the business, who is jeopardizing us all with a . . . sideline. He has to be stopped before public exposure. That would ruin all of us."

I shook my head. "Not interested, Mr. Falcone. My granddad always taught me that a man has to shoot his own dog when it goes bad. You go home and shoot yours."

Falcone looked up at me. "Mr. Heller, this newcomer is selling children."

I sat back down.

3

I got the distinct, if unstated, impression that Falcone's objections and presumably those of his fellow brothel owners concerned not the activity of child abuse but the consequences to themselves if or when this newcomer was caught. And I guess they were entitled to their own reasons for disapproval. Me, I had my own.

Over drinks, which I broke down and offered the son of a bitch, he explained in greater detail.

"This man, Carl," we were back on a first-name basis now, "is running an operation that on the surface is perfectly ordinary and legal. Naturally, like all of us, he had to undergo a very thorough investigation before he was granted a license. The county sheriff issues the licenses and conducts the investigations, not only of the person, who has to be completely clean, but of the source of his financing as well." Falcone smiled slightly. "There are ways to hide a great deal that one does not want known, of course."

There always are.

"Personally, I would have thought there's enough profit potential in our business to satisfy anyone," Falcone said, "but this, uh, person is a little more difficult to please.

"You can take my word for it that there is no problem finding employees eager to work for the income they are able to earn in the profession, but this individual does not want to pay the normal percentage even there." I noticed that he didn't say what that percentage was. And to call it a profession? You bet.

"He has a ready supply of girls from the runaway trade."

I raised my eyebrows at that one.

"You aren't familiar with it?"

"We have different areas of experience, you and I, Al."

"True enough, I suppose." He took a brief sip of the sour-mash white whiskey I get down in New Mexico, and explained. "Runaways come in all ages from preteen to the early twenties. As a rule, they're more concerned about what they left behind than what is in store for the future. Very vulnerable, almost without exception. They run away from parents, boyfriends, responsibilities, the law, whatever. They have only vague ideas about what might lie ahead, but if they think about it at all, it would normally be something glamorous. Acting, dancing, bright lights. You get the picture.

"Bus stations are the best place to find them. Nearly any major city's bus station will do, and glamor cities like Los Angeles, San Francisco, and Las Vegas are ideal. They come flocking into places like those, usually broke, convinced they're going to be discovered and become show girls or actresses or whatever. What they usually get is hepatitis and VD and street hooking, but they don't think about that at the time. They take the money out of the piggybank or whatever and get on the bus.

"Chicken hawks have a field day at the bus stations. The boys are even more vulnerable than the girls because they have less-obvious ways to earn a living.

"Anyway, this individual we are concerned about is an

expert at picking up runaways. Or he used to be. Now he generally hires others to do the work for him.

"It's easy to spot the ones who are hungry enough and gullible enough. You can promise them any damn thing. Drugs if they're already into that. Jobs. The promise of a job is the best angle. The trick is to make it not so glamorous-sounding that it makes them suspicious. So you promise them a job as a nude dancer instead of a show girl, or a streetcorner flower seller instead of an actress. Something like that." Falcone paused to take another sip of the excellent whiskey. I couldn't help but notice that he knew an awful lot about how to go about snagging runaways.

"Some of the girls he turns out himself."

"Turns loose, you mean?"

Falcone smiled. "Hardly. Turn-out is an expression in the trade. It means starting a new girl in the business. Most of the larger houses, including mine, have a girl who is a TO specialist. She trains the new girls and helps them get started on the right foot."

Gee, how thoughtful. I said nothing. The education I was getting was more than I really wanted.

"Anyway, the girls who are of age, and can prove it, he might turn out in his own legal house. The shy ones are particularly good for that. Once he gets them started, they'll stick practically without pay so no one back home will ever find out.

"The underage girls are sold, cash on the barrelhead."

I guess my eyebrows went up again.

"There are illegal specialty houses here and there, Carl, and there are, um, private collectors, you might call them.

Individuals with the money and the tastes to require fresh flesh from time to time."

"Specialty houses? Private collectors? What . . . ?"

Falcone shrugged. "They might be put to any use. It is difficult, after all, to pay even a hungry girl enough to let herself be put on a rack and whipped. There are quite a few men who go in for that sort of thing. Twelve-year-old virgins available for deflowering are not easy to come by. You have heard of snuff films?"

I nodded. They were all the rage a few years ago, women being put to death—at least allegedly—on film.

"There are a number of men, and a few women too, who are interested in participating instead of viewing." He took another sip. "Runaways can have many uses."

Falcone was explaining it all quite calmly. Personally, I gave some thought to getting sick. Jesus!

Yet, in his scummy, scuzzy corner of society it all seemed perfectly normal.

"And you are telling me that this guy is doing things like that?"

"Selling the runaways, yes. I know for sure he is doing that as a normal part of his business. There is also a videotape cassette that is supposed to have come from him. I could show it to you if you want."

"I don't want," I said quickly.

"Suit yourself," Falcone said primly. I wondered just how he had come by that kind of tape. If he might be a "collector" of specialty items himself.

"As you can well imagine, our political opponents would have entirely too much ammunition to use against the rest of us if this individual were discovered. And frankly, we do not think the man is bright enough to keep his activities undercover, where they belong."

Where they belong? Jesus!

"The man is greedy. Much too much so. We are concerned about him. We would like you to do something about him, Carl, before he does something stupid enough to hurt us."

Saying no wasn't quite as easy now as it had been a little while ago. "What about the cops?" It seemed an obvious enough question.

"That has already been tried, actually. Discreet suggestions were made. Information was filtered toward official agencies. The reaction," he made a face, "was that this recently investigated gentleman was already proved clean. It was suggested that his new establishment is taking business away from us. From me in particular. They believe I'm trying to eliminate competition."

I grunted. It could have happened that way. It could also be that Falcone was lying—he hardly came across as the most upstanding sort of fella—and simply wanted nothing to do with the law.

There was another equally obvious question that I didn't know exactly how to phrase. The hell with it. I couldn't see much reason to protect the man's sensitivities, if any.

"What about the mob?"

This time Al's smile was very small indeed. "Haven't you heard? There is no mob. Or syndicate. Or Mafia."

"I've heard that," I said. "I've also heard that there are simple and direct solutions to certain, uh, problems. So to speak."

"*If* such a thing were possible, and of course it is not, except in the imaginations of journalists and certain uninformed writers," Falcone said, "but just supposing such a thing, it might be that there are conflicts of interest."

"Financial conflicts of interest?" I asked.

Falcone smiled. "When one is using imagination, anything is possible. Even that."

Which made things somewhat clearer. I think. If I was reading him correctly, it was a matter of the people who had that kind of power not wanting to kill their own golden geese. The money, I thought, must be very large indeed. And the greed even larger, or they would have come to Falcone's conclusions about the dangers of allowing the creep to stay in business. I shook my head.

"What we want from you, Carl," Falcone said, "is some assistance. We want you to find a way to stop the trade without the kind of explosion that would create public interest. As I said before, we will pay you well. We fully understand that you normally do not accept fees. What we offer is a guarantee against all expenses and a minimum gift of ten thousand dollars simply for making an attempt on our behalf, fifty thousand if the attempt is successful."

The money itself was tempting. I like it as well as the next fellow, after all. I'm just not hung up on the subject.

The thing that made it impossible for me to say no again was the thought of what was going on.

Assuming that such things actually do go on. Al's unfriendly cops could have been right to begin with. Hell, they knew the creep better than I could after a few minutes of talking with him. Maybe it was just a fancy way to eliminate competition.

Or maybe not.

I didn't think I wanted to wake up tomorrow and face myself in the shaving mirror if I wasn't willing to find out if

Al Falcone was lying. The risks—to a whole bunch of runaway somebodies that I would never meet—were just too great for that.

"One thing, Al."

"Yes?"

"I don't want you thinking you've bought yourself a boy. You haven't. I'd tumble you just as quick as I would this scum if I found a reason for it and a way to do it."

"So we understand," Falcone said. "And we are not at all interested in your approval. Only your performance."

I sighed. I wasn't looking forward to this. I get no joy from ugliness. But I've never learned to close my eyes and pretend that there is no ugliness, either. "All right, Al. I'll take a look at it."

He nodded as if he had expected exactly that, and maybe he had. Maybe their inquiries about soft-touch Carl Heller had shown them exactly which buttons should be pushed to give them the desired results. Which proved nothing about whether Falcone was telling the truth or not. Either way, I wanted to know.

4

"When are you leaving?" Walter asked.

I have a reputation for being a closemouthed so-and-so, but that is partially a lie. There is very little that I keep from Walter, who is a friend as well as a neighbor.

Walter is in his mid-seventies and twice retired, but he's as busy as a man half his age, which, come to think of it, is just about where I fit in. Anyhow, when he is off traveling or visiting his ladyfriend down in Denver—she refuses to live in the country, and he wouldn't consider city dwelling—I take care of his place for him. He returns the favor anytime I want or need to be away from home.

"That's kind of up to you," I told him.

"I have nothing planned," he said. "Even if I did, it would have to be something rather important to interfere with this trip."

I mused out loud, "My mares aren't due to foal for about a month or six weeks, but I don't know how long this might take. The sooner the better, I expect."

"I can't imagine anything happening over there that I couldn't handle," Walter said. "You have enough hay on hand?"

I nodded. The only animals I keep in the horse trap and feed over the winter are the pregnant mares. Everything else is turned out and expected to earn its own living. I had more than enough hay to last them until the green-up. "I'll just open the gate to the stack," I said. "That way you won't even have to check that. Just keep an eye on the water from time to time." The horses in the one enclosed pasture on my place have to depend on well water. All the other stock can reach surface water, winter or summer. Like I said, I do things the old-fashioned way. Also known as the lazy man's method of ranching.

"Is there anything else I could do to help?" Walter asked. He sounded as if his interest was more than just politeness or even friendship this time. I got the impression he was taking a personal interest in it. I asked him.

"Damn right I'm interested. My brother's granddaughter ran away from home last fall, you know."

He had told me at the time, but I had forgotten about it until now.

"A pretty child. You never met her, of course, but . . . Wait a minute." He left his chair and disappeared toward his bedroom. While he was gone I helped myself to a couple Coors Lights from his refrigerator and popped open one for each of us.

When he came back, Walter showed me a small photograph that was obviously a high-school-graduation picture. It was of an attractive teenage girl with honey-blond hair and dimples. She looked like the kind of kid who would belong in a Pepsi commercial.

"They haven't heard from her since she left," he said, "and when you were telling me what that mafioso cretin said about the runaways, Carl, I . . . couldn't help but wonder. If something like that happened to her . . ."

I nodded. I knew what he was thinking. All too well.

There are some ugly sons of bitches running loose, and the more of them we can rope and castrate, the better off the world is going to be.

Walter put the picture into his pocket and seemed to be trying to put aside the thoughts that went with it. Changing the subject, he asked, "Do you have any idea what you'll do when you get there?"

"None," I admitted. "But I have a name to work on. That right there is the hardest part."

Falcone had also left me five thousand in cash toward expenses, and a telephone number, not his own, that he said would produce instant assistance, whatever my emergency might be. I didn't know quite how far to believe that, but it was an interesting thought anyway. With any amount of luck, I wouldn't have to find out how accurate the man had been on the subject.

I yawned, even though it was still fairly early in the evening. "If you don't mind, then," I said, "I think I'll take off in the morning."

"Don't worry about a thing back here, Carl. And if you need me, call."

It was no idle offer, either. If I called, that old man would come running, and he'd still be capable of doing a man-sized job when he got there. He and his ugly old Appaloosa gelding are a tough old pair, and I can't hardly wear either of them down.

"Thanks, Walter. I won't forget." I told him good night and headed home to pack my Krausers.

There are any number of ways to get from central Colorado to western Nevada. The quickest and easiest, of course, is by air, and I certainly had the bankroll to travel any way I wanted. The reason I chose the bike was because I damn well wanted to travel that way. A matter of desire rather than necessity.

This past winter had not been particularly hard, but snowpack and sudden storms make for lousy riding, so it had been quite a while since I had spent any real amount of time on two wheels.

That was particularly galling since I'd replaced my bashed in old R90 with a spanking-new R100RS Beemer— BMW to the uninitiated—while the winter sales were on. That had given me time to send the engine off to the good folks at San José for one of their full Sport Pac modifications—which makes a swift machine even swifter—and to install a fork brace. But it sure hadn't let me get out on the road to see how the trick little beastie was going to perform. With the roads clear and dry and spring warmth just around the corner, I was more than ready to try the new Beemer's wings.

Aside from being probably the best-built motorcycle alive and the most durable too, the RS model is one of the best-*looking* things ever built by mortal man. Sleek and clean lined with a full wind-tunnel fairing, low bars, and factory rearsets, the one I had grabbed off of Doc's showroom was a gleaming, soft cherry red in color. It made me feel good just to look at it, and riding an RS is about as close to spread-wing soaring as I ever expect to come.

Anyway, I was eager for that pleasure. I felt a twinge of guilt about taking a slower form of transportation than a 727, but I put that aside as quickly as it came. Speed is dandy in its place, but it is way out-of-place when you're trying to work a deal on a bad dude like this bastard was supposed to be. I was going to have to leave all of my anxieties at home and concentrate on doing this one right rather than quickly.

I packed the Krauser bags with the necessities of life—primarily cash—and a few personal items—primarily a Smith & Wesson M59, which I devoutly hoped would not turn from the latter into the former category—and latched them onto the glossy sides of my interstate-legal steed. Come morning, I buckled on the Vetterlite helmet with its ducky, light-sensitive face shield (another of the wonders of chemistry that I will never be able to comprehend beyond acknowledging that the things actually do change color when the light level changes) and fired up the tubes.

I let the Beemer warm up for a few minutes, then blasted off for US 50 by way of Lake George and Buena Vista.

Somebody, I figured, was going to pay hell before I saw home again.

5

I had been to Reno before, rodeoing there when I was young and foolish, but it had been a while. I came into Carson City on the rollercoaster that is US 50 over that way, endlessly up and down over the high desert hills that the local folks call mountains, and turned north the few miles up to Reno on 395.

When Falcone had begun telling me about his unpleasant

competitor, I had just naturally assumed he was talking about a Vegas deal. Vegas and sin seem to fit together so well, after all. But it had turned out it was Reno he was talking about instead.

It seemed logical enough in a backhanded sort of way once I thought about it. For a wide open, day-and-night-casino kind of place, Reno is more of a family-oriented spot than Las Vegas. You expect hoods on the streetcorners in Vegas—and sometimes you find them—but Reno is full of pops with hairy chests, moms with overflowing shorts, and sunburned kids entertaining themselves at pools and video-game parlors while the grown folks gamble away their vacation money. It just isn't a sinful style on display there. And where you don't expect nastiness, it is so easy to hide the same.

Prostitution isn't legal in Reno itself, so a sort of Cathouse Row has developed along the Truckee River across the line in Storey County. The famous—or infamous—Mustang Ranch has been there for years. Beyond it is Al Falcone's Falcon's Nest, slightly smaller but somewhat more elegant than the Mustang, according to its proud owner, and beyond that a place called the Red Hat Ranch, operated by a gentleman named Anthony Littori. It was the Red Hat that I was interested in.

The new Beemer brought me within reach of it within a day and a half, and that is fairly rapid transportation considering the distances involved.

The RS turned out to be every bit as much of a pleasure to ride as I'd been hoping for. Every bit as quick as my old R90 had been and much smoother at high speed.

The slick-looking fairing is low enough to give you just enough wind on the chest at high speed that it takes the pressure off the wrists at, say, seventy-five or above. Naturally I wouldn't exactly admit to speeding. But if I did do such a thing, the RS would have been real comfortable cruising at ninety or thereabouts. If I'd been interested in that sort of riding. If.

I hit the city traffic of Reno in mid-afternoon and, wonder of wonders, was still able to feel that I had a hind end, a testament to the quality of the saddle some bright soul had mounted on the bike.

Downtown areas hold little enchantment for me, so I sliced through the maze of station wagons and campers and took the freeway past the airport to the high-rise sprawl of the MGM, which hadn't been there the last time I was over this way. If Falcone was going to bankroll me for this visit, I might as well do it up in style, after all.

There are more than a few places that are prejudiced against two-wheeled transportation, but here the bellman didn't blink when I zipped to a halt under the huge, light-hung canopy at the entrance. He loaded the Krausers and tank bag onto a cart and whisked them out of sight with a nod and a smile. I didn't have to think about them again until they reappeared in my room a little while later. Service. There's something to be said for it, indeed.

I refused the offer of valet parking, satisfied myself that the Beemer was as secure as could be, and went inside to register.

Damn! The chandeliers in the place are bigger than my living room back home, and they ain't lying when they call it the Grand.

Plant grass in the casino area and there would be room enough to pasture several head of stock on it. I mean it is *big*.

Even while I was checking in I could hear the omni-present sounds of the slots busily doing their thing a few yards away. Bells ringing to draw attention to the fact that some folks do get some back now and then. The clatter of coins spilling into metal pans when the machines pay back—a very clever touch, those steel troughs; the money just sounds so damn *good* dropping into them—and the low, steady buzz and hum of a hundred excited conversations. It was wild, I'll tell you.

The room was big enough to subdivide, and the bed, naturally, was king sized. The view out the window showed the distant glitter of downtown and, far beyond, a jagged, white reminder that they do have some genuine mountains out this way. They call them the Sierras, and they are spectacular even by Colorado standards.

Open road running on a fast bike is glorious, but it does leave you kind of wind dried and gritty, so I spent some time wallowing around in the bedroom-sized bathroom before I changed and went down to admire the casino from closer range.

Lights and glitter and excitement are the order of the day there. Ranks of slot machines march off into the distance like an army of colorful tin soldiers. Carousels of dollar slots form circles topped by light boards showing the current jackpot payoff, which keeps rising a few cents at a time. The busiest of them boasted a possible payback of $634,000 and change while I was there, against a $3 play. There was a waiting line for a machine in that group.

Down one side of the long casino was green felt by the acre, broken down into small islands of the stuff at tables devoted to blackjack, craps, roulette, and wheels of fortune. Only about a third of those were busy in the afternoon.

One entire end of the huge casino was given to a massive keno board and row after row of plush, comfortable-looking chairs with writing surfaces and keno tickets conveniently at one's elbow. Lighted flashboards to display the randomly selected keno numbers were located throughout the casino and in the restaurants surrounding it.

Separate playing areas squirted off to the sides for poker, sporting events, and what have you.

All in all, the place was overwhelming.

And it took me a few minutes, but eventually I realized that throughout the hotel, in the hallways leading to the rooms, in the shops, and in the restaurants, there were photographs and posters reminding one of the appeal of the great MGM film stars of the past. Everywhere, that is, except in the casino. There there were no distractions from the principal order of business, which was the gambling.

On the casino floor the atmosphere was so elegantly greedy that I was having trouble adjusting to it, like I had gone through some sort of time warp and had landed unexpectedly on foreign territory.

I swallowed hard, but it was no simple altitude change that was filling my ears and threatening to fog my brain; and to give myself some time to make the changeover from dry wind to fevered gambling, I headed for the relative peace of the nearest of the several restaurants.

Even there the gambling was pervasive, if not quite so frenzied, because there were keno runners—intense young girls with short skirts and mouth-watering lengths of attractive leg—whisking among the tables to accept bets against the keno boards that flashed just above eye level in any direction one might look.

Rebelling against the elegance of it all, I plunked myself at a table and ordered a plebeian hamburger and fries. I was almost disappointed when it turned out to be the best damn burger I'd had in a long, long while.

6

It felt almost strange riding a bare bike after more than a thousand miles of being encumbered with luggage, but it was a pleasure to take the rising and falling sweepers of Interstate 80 along the Truckee Valley east of Reno. It was the tag end of the day, but there was plenty of light to see the sharply distinctive line of bright green foliage along the river and, in extreme contrast, the barren, dry, high-desert hillsides only yards beyond that lush riverbank border.

I never saw a marker showing when I entered Storey County, but I knew I was there when I passed the turnoff to the Mustang. There is even a marked exit for it on the interstate, although as far as I could determine there was no town or post office to justify the named exit. Just a bar and trailer camp on one side of the highway and a collection of junkyards and the whorehouse on the river side.

A small sign off the right-of-way pointed toward the Falcon's Nest beyond the Mustang and, past that, the Red Hat. I chopped the throttle and let the shaft drive of the RS squat in deceleration.

A gravel road snaked away from the highway toward the cool green of the river, and I felt a twinge of nervousness when I followed it. I'd have thought I would have outgrown such crap a long time ago, but I hadn't. A visit to a whorehouse *should* have been a guilt-making experience, and the fact that it was perfectly legal here made no impression at all on my gut reactions. The flavor was definitely illicit, regardless of official approval.

I couldn't comment on all of Nevada's brothels, not having seen them, but this one was an impressive and rather imposing sight.

A long, paved parking area flanked by carefully groomed plantings greeted the visitor. Off to the side was an even larger gravel area with a sign indicating that it was for truck parking. Long haulers welcomed and apparently frequently, I gathered.

A tall fence of wrought iron topped with wicked-looking spear points surrounded another expanse of groomed and professionally tended grounds.

The "house" itself was a sprawling, pseudo-Spanish style of architecture with fake adobe walls and a red tile roof. Oddly—or perhaps not so oddly, come to think of it— the lines of the building were disrupted by a watchtower jutting up above the center line of the roof. The thing reminded me of the shotgun towers that surround the walls of the old territorial prison in Canon City. Once a fellow was in there, I gathered, he would not get out without the management's approval. I tucked that thought away.

Getting in was not entirely casual either. A wrought-iron gate at least eight feet tall blocked the sidewalk. A little sign beside it instructed the guest to push the button for entry. I pushed the button.

The loud buzz of an electric lock was the response, and I was able to push open the gate. I stepped through and couldn't help but notice that the thing swung shut behind me with a very solid clang.

A Hispanic gardener was bent over some shrubbery beside the path leading to the massive front doors. He glanced my way when I came up the walk but avoided making eye contact. Disapproval? I wondered. Or disinterest?

Falcone hadn't prepared me for going through that door, and I wished that he had.

Hell, I was already nervous and uncomfortable enough without embarrassment being added to it.

I stepped through the door—no buzzer this time—and was faced by a solid wall of flesh.

Girls, a dozen of them or maybe more, lined up as if for inspection. Bathing suits and high heels. Tall and short, scrawny to chunky, raw merchandise on display.

There was simply too much of it there to permit individual attention. It was like being hit in the face by it.

To make it all the more confusing, there was a long-haired, grubby-looking man probably in his mid-twenties sitting on a stool beside the entrance. He didn't do a hell of a lot to put me at ease.

"Pick a girl."

"What?"

"Pick a girl," he repeated.

I was still trying to adjust to the visual and emotional impact of all that meat. "I don't know—"

"You don't wanta pick a girl?" he interrupted. In a louder voice he called, "He doesn't wanta pick a girl."

The lineup broke into individual segments, and the whores slouched away with bored expressions.

I turned to ask the guy what the procedure was supposed to be here, but it was too late for that. He had already left his stool and was disappearing through a doorway with a sign above it saying it was for employees only.

Nice folks, I thought somewhat sourly.

Since I was virtually alone in the big room then, I took a moment to regain some lost senses.

The place was . . . plush. And bright scarlet red. Plush red carpet. Flocked red wallpaper. Red velvet couches. Luminous red on black velvet paintings of nudes on the walls. Rose-shaded teardrop crystals in the chandelier overhead.

It was, I suppose, everything a fellow could ask a whorehouse to be.

Off to the right was a small sign reading BAR. I headed that way.

I won't say that I exactly recognized any of the faces or the bodies that went with them as being the girls who had just been in the lineup, but there were a bunch of girls in there. There was also a male bartender, who looked big enough to bulldog real bulls instead of little old Mexican steers, and a couple quiet customers drinking at the mahogany bar. The girls seemed to be ignoring everyone, including one another.

"What do you want?" the bartender asked.

"Time," I said. "And a Coors Light."

He delivered the Coors, which I figured also bought me the time, and accepted four bucks in return. That price was not enough to buy me a smile or a welcome, just the beer.

Real nice folks here, I was thinking.

I took a swallow and wondered if I would be approached by one of the unoccupied girls. I wasn't. They seemed quite willing to pretend that I didn't exist. And maybe I didn't at that, as far as they were concerned. Not, at least, until I had my wallet out. Why any sensible male would subject himself to this kind of crap I could not imagine.

At least the drink did buy me the time I wanted to get a look around and the adjustment period I needed. Not wanted so much as needed, actually.

After a few minutes the girls began to sort themselves out into individual faces and figures.

The mixture was well balanced. Anglo-Saxon gals with a preponderance of slim, youthful, blond good looks that surprised me. Black girls with cornrowed hair. Chicanas, one of whom was absolutely stunning if you didn't look at the blank, expressionless pits where her eyes should have been. A pair of incredibly tiny Orientals with hair streaming down below waist level and no figures to speak of. I thought their hair might weigh more than the rest of their lilliputian bodies.

All of them were wearing high-heeled shoes and form-fitting bathing suits of a translucent material that let their nipples be seen clearly. All in all a pretty raw display.

A doorbell chimed from somewhere toward the entry, and a male voice called out, "Company, girls."

The whores left the bar and moved lazily toward the big entry room, and others appeared from side corridors to form into another lineup. All of them, I saw, had expressions that were devoid of any interest in what was going on around them.

I carried my beer out to watch the cattle call and got there in time to see one of the whores in the middle of the line lean forward to peer at the newly arrived customer coming down the walkway. She turned to the girl beside her and made a face, saying something too low for me to hear. Whatever it was brought a short, mean bark of derisive laughter from the other girl.

Yeah, I thought, they really like and respect the guys they service here. You bet.

The man came in, an elderly Oriental whose clothes said he could afford plenty of time at the Red Hat and at the gaming tables too, and the girl who had been making the remarks smiled.

The customer took his time about inspecting the beef, then made a circular motion with his hand.

"Turn around, girls," the creep on the stool called.

They did. Only a few of them bothered to go to the trouble of striking poses for the display. Most of them just slouched from one position to the other as directed.

"Turn," the creep said, and they faced the guy.

The customer stepped forward and held out his hand to a slim and actually quite pretty blond girl who looked like she should be a high-school cheerleader instead of a Red Hat hooker.

The blonde's expression did not change at all, and instead of stepping forward to greet the man who was about to pay for the privilege of screwing her, she stepped backward and walked the length of the lineup behind the other girls before she joined him and led him into one of the branching corridors off the inspection room or whatever the hell they called it.

I couldn't help but shake my head. That poor bastard would probably have as good a time making love to his own five fingers as he would get from sweet blondie.

"Something wrong, cowboy?"

"What?"

The whores were filing out of the room past me, and one had stopped beside me without my noticing it until she spoke.

"Disappointed?" she asked.

I shrugged. "It's just so impersonal."

She smiled. "We don't get personal until we get to a room, cowboy. Would you like to go to my room?"

7

I was kind of surprised. Not that she had asked, of course. That was what she was here for. What I hadn't really expected was my own reaction.

The girl was a pretty thing, tall and tanned and willowy. Her hair was light brown, worn short and softly curling. She had the prettiness and the same kind of winsome appeal to remind me strongly of Dorothy Hamill of Olympic skating fame a few years ago, and I've always thought that that young lady was one of the most delightful girls to come down the pike into public attention in many a moon.

Any healthy male in his right mind would want to cuddle up close to a girl that attractive.

Yet, looking into the flat, fake phoniness that was this look-alike's smile and into the emptiness that was in her eyes, all the comparisons were washed away and I felt a vague, visceral sense of revulsion at the thought of allowing her flesh to touch mine.

It wasn't a matter of cleanliness, either. Hell, these girls are given health checks weekly and I'm told are careful about their customers too.

It wasn't a matter of use. I've spent many a fun hour romping with women whose attitudes on the subject would be considered liberal, to put it the most charitable way possible.

I've even had professionals sicced on me a time or two in the past and never gave much thought to it except to go along for the ride and enjoy the experience without fretting about it.

This was something else entirely.

It was just so damned . . . cold.

These whores were not even making a *pretense* of giving.

They simply didn't give a shit about the poor guys who came here looking for comfort, finding instead a soulless hustle that left only themselves doing the giving. And that only of money.

Personally, I've always believed that the business of prostitution performs a valuable public service. Whores were the first practicing psychologists, and I guess a good one still can be. They can give a form of comfort to the lonely that has sex as its excuse but not its reason.

But these people weren't offering anything like that. They weren't even trying to. They just didn't care.

I sighed and looked at the empty shell that should have been a very pretty girl.

I'd had in mind some vague notion of getting acquainted

with one of the Red Hat girls and trying to worm into the place that way. Not a plan, really, just a half-formed idea.

But after seeing these scuzzes at work, there was no way I was going to go to one of the rooms and spill my seed into one of these unreachable mannequins.

I value myself too highly for that, by damn.

"No," I told her.

The whore shrugged, and her face went back to that masklike indifference that they all seemed to wear around here. "Suit yourself, cowboy."

Sexually I just wasn't interested, but I was curious about why she kept calling me "cowboy." Maybe she was more perceptive than I was giving her credit for, because at the moment I was wearing slacks and a polo shirt and motorcycle-touring boots instead of my usual Stetson and high-heeled Justins.

"Wait a minute."

"Yeah?" She stopped and turned, her eyes flicking up and down in an obvious assessment of both my presumed interest and probable ability to pay.

Instead of changing my mind about the trip to the room, though, I asked her about that "cowboy" business.

She tossed her head a little and managed to give the impression that she was chewing a cud of gum even though she was not. "I call everybody that, mister."

I think it might have startled her, at least a tiny bit, that my reaction was a broad grin and a feeling of great relief. "Thanks," I said. I meant it, too. It did me good to find out that the witch was no more sensitive or perceptive than I'd been giving her credit for. "Thanks a lot."

She gave me a look of mild disgust and turned away.G

Gee, I was sorry to see her go. We'd been having such a swell time.

I finished my beer, watched two more lineups while I was doing so, and finally snagged the long-haired creep before he darted back into whatever dank cave he stayed in when he was not directing a cattle auction.

"I want to talk to Mr. Littori," I told him.

His expression was as blank as the whores'. "Mr. Littori doesn't entertain the customers. You want a girl, pick one. You don't want a girl, get outta here. It's that simple."

For a moment I had this real nifty vision of how the creep would look if I kind of sliced his Adam's apple with the edge of my hand. It is a downright effective method of getting a man's attention, and it was awfully tempting. Wouldn't take hardly any time at all.

On the other hand, this was one very secure piece of real estate, and I'd already made enough of a bad start to this business by coming here pretending to be a customer. It seemed impolitic to compound the problem now.

So I let the son of a bitch go on breathing in the normal manner.

I was also getting the germ of an idea about how I might best go about causing some trouble for the estimable gentleman who operated this crummy palace.

"Tell Mr. Littori that a gentleman named Carl Heller was here to see him. Tell him I asked politely for an interview. Do that for me, would you? *Chum?*" I let the last word sound like I was cussing him, which I guess I was.

"Fuck off," he said pleasantly.

"Not with these scags," I said just as nicely.

I let myself out and will admit to being pleased to find that the door opened when I wanted it to.

8

I made a call to the telephone number Al Falcone had given me and reached an anonymous voice that confirmed I was supposed to get any assistance I required. I required some. After, a few minutes of my explaining, the voice said, "Give us two days. The word will be out by that time. You should know that it will reach ears other than Fat Tony's."

"Fat Tony is Littori?"

"Yeah."

"Just so it reaches him."

I could almost hear the guy shrug. "Tony. The cops. Just so you know it, pal."

"I know it. Thanks."

I hung up the phone and stood to stretch. After my conversation I felt taller. And leaner. And damn well meaner than I'd been feeling all the long winter long. I felt pretty damn good, in fact. And Tony Littori had better watch his butt, because I did intend to chew on it some.

Still, I had a couple days to kill now, according to the gentleman on the telephone, and even I can't sleep all that away. Since I was rooming only nine floors above one of the country's finer casinos—and since I had a gaudy wad of disposable cash in my hip pocket—the logical thing to do would be to go enjoy some of it. I took the elevator down with growing visions of having the nice people at the MGM Grand fatten my bank account.

By now it was late enough that anywhere else in the US of A people would be thinking of calling it a night, but you couldn't tell that from the activity in the casino.

People milled all through the huge room, big enough, I thought, to swallow Mile High Stadium at a single gulp, and the sounds of the slots were everywhere. The crank and whir of the bandit arms. The bells. The metallic clatter of falling coins. It was infectious.

I've never thought of myself as a gambler. Not the money kind of gambling anyway.

Oh, you can't hardly spend any time on the rodeo circuit without playing a bit. But I never went in for it much. Dice have always left me cold, and too many of the boys go nuts with wild cards and strange versions of the basically straightforward and decent game that poker used to be, so I played just enough to be sociable and always left it at that.

Here things were just a *leetle* bit different from the way they are out behind the chutes.

Slot machines, I am told, have the poorest payback of any of the casino games. We all know that. On a purely intellectual level. The simple truth is that the damn things also offer the most fun and excitement.

So I cheerfully played the flatland tourister chump and had a change girl swap me a gaggle of cartwheels for a fifty-dollar bill that Al Falcone had put into my pocket.

It is something of a pity, but even those alloy Eisenhower sandwich dollar coins are disappearing from the casinos. The treasury department's unlamented foolishness with the Susan B. Anthony has made the big dollars scarce too, so nowadays the casinos are issuing their own nonnegotiable tokens for the dollar slots. The fact that their size and weight are the same as an Eisenhower, and that the real minted coin will also work in the slots, is theoretically a coincidence, I believe.

Anyway, the change girl provided me with a double handful of the dollar gaming tokens, which showed the roaring MGM lion on one side and an engraving of the hotel on the other. She also gave me a sturdy paper cup to carry it all in.

I must say that after the indifference of the people out at the Red Hat, the cheerfulness of the staff at the hotel was a joy. I never got anything but a smile there, and never received change that wasn't accompanied by a truly genuine-sounding wish that I have good luck.

The high-pot carousels were so busy that it would have been difficult to find a free machine at one, and anyway I'm not particularly keen on the idea of throwing it away by the handful. A buck at a time is enough for me to have fun, so I poked around until I found a progressive machine with five wheels and a left–right read for the payback.

The machine would take five coins at a time, but I dropped a single buck into it and pulled on the lever. There was a satisfying little chunk as each of the wheels locked to a stop, and a cherry showed up on the far right spinner. Ching-chink! Two dollars dropped into the pan at the bottom of the machine. If I'd played five coins I would have gotten back ten. On the other hand, the percentage was the same regardless. And hell, I'd rather have the fun of watching the wheels spin five times than just once. I dropped another coin—excuse me, token—into the bandit and watched an MGM lion intrude on what would otherwise have been a delightful line of plums. So close that time. I grinned at my own gullibility and dropped another buck into the machine.

A half-hour later I was down by half a cup of dollars but still had most of a bourbon and water, delivered free fer nuthin' by a smilingly efficient young fellow in a red vest and bow tie. The drinks come gratis, and I was more than surprised when I realized that in spite of that, there were no drunks around. The customers came to play, I guessed, instead of imbibe. Whatever the reason, there seemed to be no problem with it, and I thought it was a nice touch.

Still, my arm was getting a bit tired from all that work, so I gathered up my coins and drink and drifted away to see what else was going on around me.

I stopped to watch an Oriental couple—it seemed that half the players were Oriental these days, which I hadn't seen in the joints I'd gone to when I was here for the annual rodeo a long while back—win a healthy pile of five-dollar chips at the roulette wheel, then sat in for a while at a two-dollar to one-thousand-dollar blackjack table.

The dealer was crisply neat in a long-sleeved white shirt and black tie but much more intent and much less smiling than most of the other casino employees. I played for forty minutes or so and built my investment nearly back to its original level before I decided to go try something else.

I hadn't been down to the far end of the casino toward the sports-book room, closed at this time of night, so I headed that way.

There were the inevitable slots, of course, including a raised platform area where the jackpot was supposed to include world tours and private aircraft and all manner of goodies. Oddly enough, there was practically no one down in that end of the place, except for a couple of players in that brightly lighted raised area and a change girl to see that they had the wherewithal to plug the machines.

The theater for the big stage extravaganza was down that way too, but the doors were closed, and if anything was going on inside there at the moment I couldn't see or hear it.

I yawned—it was getting late enough that I was afraid to look at my watch for fear I would be ashamed of myself—and idled down the rows of slots looking for a progressive dollar machine. Most of the ones I was passing at the moment were nickel and quarter machines.

"Don't! Please don't, sir, or I'll have to call security and . . ."

"A hundred bucks, girlie."

The first voice was feminine, the second masculine. The words were followed by the distinct sound of a face being slapped. I sighed and set my cup of coins beside the nearest slot.

They were on the far side of a tall bank of nickel slots. When I stepped around to see what was going on—well, that was obvious; to see what I might be able to do about it, then—there was a leggy keno runner in her black-and-red working costume being groped by a fellow who looked like he'd had about one too many.

The silly bastard looked like he should have been out in the camper with ma and the kids. Hardly a masher type in his shorts and sandals and dark blue socks, but I guess a combination of free liquor and gambling disappointment had rearranged his expectations of what the staff ought to be willing to do to give him solace. Whatever the reason, he was giving the girl a hard time.

"Naughty, naughty," I told him softly.

Since I'd come up behind him in a perfect position for it,

I reached out and took hold of his shoulder, with my fingertips taking a bite into that sensitive hollow inside the collarbone. Judging from the way he went pale all of a sudden, I would say that it kinda hurt. Which it was supposed to do.

The guy looked no more harmful than a disgruntled Milquetoast, and I fully expected him to wilt or whimper or try to pull away.

Instead, he made a rapid and damn well skillful shuffle back toward me and drove the point of an elbow into my belly just below the breastbone.

I gave out a *whuff* that was partly escaping air and partly pain and decided that the gentleman was maybe not so helpless as I'd been thinking.

So much for gentle persuasions. While I still had some oxygen in the system to feed the muscles, I gave him my very best, A-number-one shot to the kidney.

I knew good and well that he would be one anxious, worried fella the next few times he took a leak, and he just had to be hurting, but he *still* wasn't ready to quit.

He spun and threw a real wingdinger of a right so quick I couldn't block it. I was lucky to deflect it enough that it scraped across my temple instead of landing flush, and even that was enough to bring water to my left eye and sting like hell.

Enough of this noise, I thought, and waded into him, good and mad by now and flinging a flurry of down-low body punches hard enough that they would take the starch out of a bull elk.

My superior physical conditioning, quick wit, and moral righteousness—coupled with the fact that the guy was already half-looped—melted him down onto his knees, where he seemed to be more interested in trying not to retch up his drinks than in doing any more tussling.

That was fine by me. I bent over and began doing some thinking about getting back my breath. The ability to suck air seemed to have gone away for a little while there.

The next thing I knew, I was bent over backward with both arms locked in a tidily applied come-along, and these two fellows in gray shirts were whispering in my ear.

9

"Does it hurt?" she asked.

I shook my head, and she reached across the small green table to touch the abrasion gently. The security people had dabbed some antiseptic on the spot and more or less—mostly less—thanked me for helping out before they got there. The girl had apparently felt there should be some further effort of thanks made. The coffee was her treat.

"Tell me something," I requested.

"Of course."

"The security people. How did they know? I mean, there wasn't any noise or anything."

"The cameras."

I raised an eyebrow.

"The casino area is under TV surveillance twenty-four hours a day, every square inch of it. It's all on tape, too.

They wouldn't let you watch it or anything like that, I wouldn't think, but one of the supervisors will see it in the morning just to verify what you told them and what I said. They have to be very careful about lawsuits and things like that."

That was logical enough. An outfit rich enough to bet a million bucks against the spin of a slot wheel would be a juicy target for every con game in the known universe. That kind of vulnerability must make for very large caution.

I smiled at the girl. "I don't even know your name."

Until we got to the coffee shop I hadn't actually been paying all that much attention to her, being somewhat occupied by other thoughts, like whether I was going to have to do my explaining through a gridwork of bars, but now things were toning down some. Now that I was paying attention to her, I couldn't imagine not doing so earlier.

She was a striking young lady, but she was so damned cute that it took several looks to realize there was a lot of down-deep attractiveness beyond the cutesy appeal.

She had a short cut cap of gleaming black hair and flawlessly textured skin that was a creamy golden ivory. At first glance and for several more I'd thought she might be Hispanic, but her eyes made me question that. They were an almost startling green, and there was a hint of fold at the corners of those large, pretty eyes that was close to being Oriental. I began to wonder if being around so many Japanese tourists here was clouding my judgment on that subject.

What made her so dang cute was partially her size, which must have been shy of five feet without the high heels that went with the uniform, and mostly the actual, honest-to-

Pete dimples that showed whenever she smiled or threatened to.

Unlike the cigarette girls' costumes, which were sexy/flashy right down to blinking electric lights for earrings, the keno runners wore a rather severe red-and-black outfit that was not particularly calculated to display a figure. There must have been one under there, but I couldn't pass any judgments on it except to note that the girl's waist looked small enough to be a one-hand reach. Impossible, of course, but that was the impression given.

And she had those legs. Like the man said, they reached all the way up. Little-bitty as she was, eighty percent of her seemed to be sleek, impeccably formed leg.

All in all, she was a cute, elfin little thing who was also damn nice-looking in other ways.

"Julie," she said. She looked a bit shy. "Julie Jones. It's my real name. Honest."

I don't think I looked skeptical or confused. Hell, I was perfectly willing to accept whatever name she gave me from Rodriguez to Chang, but she went on as if it was a habit.

"In case you're wondering," she said, "and most do around here, I'm Eurasian. Half-Korean and half-GI. I was adopted. My parents are perfectly normal, perfectly marvelous white Caucasian Americans. I don't know anything about my natural parents. I don't especially want to. I had a wonderful childhood. I love my parents. I don't need therapy, sympathy, or anything in between. Okay?"

She was still smiling when she ended all of that, but she was also a little bit breathless, a little bit shy, and, I thought, more than a little bit defensive.

"Wouldn't it save time," I asked, "if you just had all that printed on a card and handed it around? Let's try this again.

You are Julie. I'm Carl." I stuck my hand out across the table, and so what if that's supposed to be a breach of proper etiquette. "I'm pleased to meet you, Julie Jones."

The shyness was still there, but she had gotten back her breath. And she didn't look quite so defensive now. She reached forward and shook hello. "All right." She grinned. "I guess I just get a little . . ."

"Tired of complete strangers thinking they have some right to your life history? I expect I can understand that."

The grin broadened. "Okay then."

"No harm, no foul, Julie."

"And I really do want to thank you for pulling that crumb off me a while ago."

I laughed. "Let me guess. He started out asking about your personal history and wanted to know more after your standard spiel, right?"

She made a face but wasn't able to avoid being cute doing it.

"And now you're beginning to wonder, since I'm just as much of a stranger as he was, if I'm going to misinterpret your gesture with the coffee and the concern and try to step in where he left off. Spoils to the victor and all that."

This time the face she made was not cute. She thought it over for a moment, then acknowledged the accuracy with a nod.

"It's good coffee," I said. "I'm enjoying it. But I don't think it's worth making you uncomfortable. Thanks for the concern too, Julie Jones." I smiled at her, stood, and laid down a bill for the tip. She had volunteered the coffee and I didn't want to take the gesture away from her, so I left the check where it was.

"Wait."

"What?"

She looked shy again. "It's been a bad night. Usually I'm not so suspicious of everybody." She smiled. "As a matter of fact, usually this is as nice a place to work as I've ever found. The customers here are better than you find most places, and usually I like them a lot. You know?"

"Sure."

"So, well, why don't you sit down and finish your coffee anyhow."

"Okay." I sat. She stirred the contents of her cup, which I didn't think should need any stirring. "Would you mind a dumb-tourist kind of question?"

"Not at all."

"This keno game that you work at. I don't understand it worth a darn."

She smiled easily, back on comfortable ground. "It's really very simple. Also very Oriental. At least an awful lot of Orientals are partial to it. A lot of others too, of course, maybe because it can be such a slow and comfortable way to lose money. You can sit in an easy chair and have people wait on you while you play. Anyway . . ."

It really was pretty simple. The board is numbered 1 to 80. Players bet that particular numbers will come up on the board. They can bet as little as a buck and pick one number or as many as fifteen. The more numbers you mark, the bigger the potential payback but the less likelihood of "catching" your numbers.

The numbers are chosen at random by a jet of forced air blowing numbered Ping-Pong balls into slots. Twenty of the eighty numbers are drawn for each game, one-quarter of the total. The maximum payback is fifty thousand dollars for a one-dollar bet, but it takes fourteen correct numbers to hit that. If you pick only one number and bet a dollar on it, you get back three dollars if your number is one of the twenty drawn. Very simple and rather slow.

"Some people play the same set of numbers year in and year out," she said. "What I do is go outside the keno area to the bars and the restaurants and like that, and collect the marked tickets and the bets. If a player wins I'll collect his winnings and take that to him too. Or her. Women like the game too. Keno and slots. You mostly find men at the tables."

"Do you play?"

She shook her head and gave me a shy grin. "Not really. Of course the only thing an employee is allowed to play here is the slots. We aren't allowed to play anything that's touched by human hands."

"I thought you told me the keno balls are in a sealed container and aren't touched."

"They aren't, but the tickets are." She shrugged. "Most of us who work here don't gamble much anyway. You came here to play because it isn't legal wherever you're from, but it isn't such a novelty to us. Where are you from, anyway?"

Now that is a subject I can talk on at some length, and I guess I did. The idea of the mountains was no particular novelty to her either, with Tahoe and the Sierras practically out the back door, and she was interested in the Longhorns. But she got all aquiver at the descriptions of the horses.

"I adore horses," she said when she finally was able to get a word in. "I've always dreamed of being able to have one of my own. Tell me more about your old mare." She glanced at her watch. "Look, before you do that, I need to go check out. They were nice enough to give me time off so I could calm down, but I don't think they want me to disappear altogether. I . . . if you wouldn't mind, that is, maybe after I clock out and change we could have breakfast or something."

"Sure." I looked at my watch and was astonished to discover that it was well into the breakfast hour. The whole night had kind of gotten away from me somehow. "I'll be right here."

"Okay." She gave me a dimpled smile and slipped gracefully out of her chair. Pretty little thing, I thought. I wondered how old she was, since I hadn't been able to come up with any reasonable guesses based on appearance. Between fifteen and thirty was about as near as I could get.

I watched her walk away and began to groan a bit at my own stupidity. I'd just remembered that many moons ago I had set a damn near full cup of dollars beside a slot machine in some dark and distant corner of the casino. By now that money was long gone.

I shook my head at my own dumbness and hoped that whoever had found it had won a bundle courtesy of Al Falcone.

10

"You are a lovely girl, Julie Jones," I told her. I meant it, too.

She smiled and sighed and nuzzled in a little closer, her fingertips trailing lightly down my stomach.

"But if I don't get some sleep pretty soon," I added, "I'm going to be most ungentlemanly and conk out cold on you here."

"We did come up here so you could get some sleep, didn't we," she mused.

"I seem to remember something like that, yes."

"You won't mind if I wake you up an hour or so before I have to go back to work, will you?"

"Two hours would be better, I think."

She showed me her dimples. "Much better."

I closed my eyes and let myself sink into the soft expanse of the rented bed. It had been a long day and a longer night, and I felt a quiet contentment now.

A phrase came into my mind. Postcoital depression. A lot of do-it-yourself psych books seem to be big on postcoital depression. I've never understood that phrase myself. Sure couldn't understand it now.

Making quiet love with a nice person is always something I've regarded as a genuine pleasure.

It leaves me contented and relaxed. Damn sure not depressed.

I've often wondered if the people who are depressed afterward are unfortunate folks who have been alone in an act that has to be shared if it is going to be anything more than a masturbatory duet. I don't mean physically alone but emotionally so.

For sure I had not been alone in this early afternoon with the drapes drawn and a pale, yellow light filtering through to fill the big room with a golden glow that may or may not have had much to do with the color of the light itself.

My pretty keno runner had turned out to be a girl who was giving and caring, and I'd found myself wanting to give back to her at least as much pleasure as she was willing to give to me. As a form of competition, that has to rank high on the list of contests worth entering. Much more important than expertise, any old time. Those scags out at the Red Hat were probably as expert as any females in the Western Hemisphere. But Julie gave a damn. I felt around and lightly kissed the nearest part of her, which turned out to be her forehead. I felt her stir a little and heard a hint of contented sigh.

Good. No postcoital depression for her either. I was glad. I felt myself floating a little closer to sleep.

I hadn't really intended to wind up in bed with the girl, and I rather doubt that it had been her intention either. Certainly she was not the type who went around hustling the customers or, I figured, bedding them.

After breakfast she had made a suggestion that I never would have expected, nor thought of on my own, but which turned out to be a helluva lot of fun.

She wanted to go bowling.

You go to Reno and you think of gambling and good times. Not bowling. But the hotel had its own alley with 2,712 lanes, more or less, and the girl liked to bowl.

It was something I hadn't done since back in my feckless student days, and only three or four times then, but I went along with it and darned if I didn't even enjoy it. Surprised me, it did. Especially since this little snip of a pretty girl could spot me twenty pins and still whup me something awful.

Still, it was fun, and I enjoyed it, and somewhere along that period of time I discovered that I really liked and enjoyed Miss Julie Jones too. The discovery seemed to work in two directions, and when finally I was so wiped out from lack of sleep that I couldn't go any further, it seemed just natural as could be that she would come along back to my room.

Natural, too, that I was not quite as wiped-out exhausted as I had thought.

Tiny as she was, Julie was one of those girls who is somehow bigger without her clothes than in them. Ripe and sweet and very busy. No reluctance to ask for the things that gave her the greatest pleasure. No reluctance to provide as much for me.

I sighed. Depressed? No way. Vastly contented, you bet.

She left the room before I did, on her way to clock in for work, her cheeks flushed slightly from recent exertions and releases, sweet curve of lips slack, eyelids droopy, knees a trifle loose in the joints. I knew how she felt or at least imagined that I did. I felt very much that way myself.

"Later, Carl?"

"If I'm very fortunate." She bent to give me a brief, chaste kiss and was gone.

I looked at my watch and discovered that it was approaching midnight. Residence in a casino hotel, it seemed, blew normal schedules all to hell and gone.

I lit a cigarette and leaned back against a mound of pillows, enjoying the lassitude and hollowness of belly that comes after really good lovemaking. Thought about going back to sleep but knew I could not. I had just awakened— well, not very long before, anyway—from an entire afternoon of snoring—Julie's claim, not mine—and had no desire for more. So I showered and dressed and went downstairs in search of food and another assault on the tables and the slots. When in Rome, and all that.

11

The lady was striking enough to meet the Hollywood image of a casino patron, unlike the reality of stuffed shorts and wrinkled Japanese that most of the customers seemed to be.

This one was a tall, slender, decidedly sensual blonde with an Audrey Hepburn neck, tightly coiffed Grace Kelly hairdo, and pale satin Lesley-Ann Down shoulders above a gown that could have been used for a Black Velvet billboard photo. So damned stunning she was theatrical, right down to the rings and bracelets and dangling diamond earrings.

Her perfume was about enough to make a grown man paw the ground and look for a matador to charge. For the past ten minutes or so she had been sitting at my left shoulder at a two-dollar blackjack table making ten-dollar bets and squealing with unconcealed delight every time she won. If it hadn't been for the pleasant, and recent, memory of Julie Jones, I think I would have been uncomfortable with her there.

As it was I turned up an ace-queen blackjack, collected three bucks back from my two-dollar bet, and watched patiently while the lady drew two cards to a bust and the dealer went on to the next player at the crowded table.

"Light?"

"Ma'am?"

"I asked would you mind lighting my cigarette."

"Of course not." I flicked the Bic for her to ignite the filtered and holder-fitted menthol thing she was smoking and moved the ashtray from my right elbow to my left so she could reach it.

"Thank you." Her voice was a throaty purr, and she had a way of moving her long-lashed eyes that made me wonder if I ought to recognize her from some screen credits.

"Yes, ma'am."

She wrinkled her nose and made a small pout with her mouth, every bit as elegantly formed as the rest of her, and asked, "Have I reached an age where gentlemen refer to me as 'ma'am'?"

I gave her a polite smile and said, "Just a country boy's habit. Ma'am."

She laughed and made it a furry, feline sound. The dealer was ready to pull cards from the shoe again, so I dragged my bet back to the two-dollar minimum and concentrated on the play. My favored spot at the table, for no particular reason that I know of, is on the far right, so I'm always the first to draw cards. This time I was dealt a nine-eight and slid the cards under the pair of dollar tokens to signify that I was done. The woman called for another card, got a seven, and stopped there. The dealer went expressionlessly on around the table. One man busted and lost his bet; the rest of us collected even money when the dealer had to draw to sixteen and pulled a six to bust.

"Shuffle," the dealer called over her shoulder.

"Why do you do that?"

"Sir?"

"Why do you call out like that every time you shuffle?"

She shrugged, still without expression. "They like to know." The cards seemed to dance under her quick fingers as she cut and shuffled and recut in the unvarying pattern. I thought about asking how many decks were in that thick pile of cards but decided not to ask. Big grins and chatter with the patrons was not this particular dealer's pot of tea.

She finished the shuffle, slid the cards together, and offered them and the plastic cut-card to the pretty lady beside me. Large stones flashed in the lights when the woman reached forward to slip the cut-card into the near end of the new deck. "Thin to win," I remembered from somewhere in the past.

Apparently it worked. I got a seven-five, drew a nine, and called that enough. Twenty-one. Hard to beat. The lady next to me looked at her cards, yelped with delight, and turned over an ace-ten blackjack. The dealer paid her three five-dollar tokens and went stonily on to the next player.

"I think you bring me luck."

"Ma'am?"

She smiled with a radiance that penetrated somewhere into my chest cavity and said, "We aren't going to start that again, are we?"

"Sorry."

"I was saying, I think you bring me luck."

"I hope you're right about that."

The next deal my seventeen lost to the dealer's twenty, but the woman had let her twenty-five dollars ride and pulled a twenty-one after a two-card draw.

"See," she said. "You definitely bring me luck."

"Good." My pile was somewhat smaller than what I had started with, and I began to rake my collection of fake dollars into a pocket.

"You aren't leaving, are you?"

I shrugged. "Since I can't whip the table I thought I'd try the slots instead."

"Would you mind some company?" Her eyelashes, very long, fluttered and fell prettily. "I know it's terribly superstitious of me, but I do think you gave me luck."

"I guess I wouldn't mind." Gamblers, I thought. For some of them the air seemed to be full of omens, good and bad alike.

"But no more of this 'ma'am' nonsense." She extended a bejeweled hand. "Sybil Stone," she said.

"Carl Heller," I said. Her fingers, lightly touched, were warm and dry, and she was in no hurry to withdraw them.

She gathered her winnings into a tiny black-velvet purse and left the table with me.

"Where are you from, Carl?"

I told her. "You?"

"Los Angeles."

"I expect I should have guessed that."

"Was that a compliment or an indictment?"

"I don't understand."

She laughed again and placed a hand lightly on my arm. We were not, I noticed, moving toward the slot machines. "Next to Texans, Carl, Californians are probably the most resented people in the country. It's all jealousy, of course, but it makes us wonder just the same."

"My intention was to compliment, not to complain," I assured her. "Coloradoans don't have to be jealous of anybody. Are you an actress?"

She beamed with pleasure and rolled her head on that fine, slim neck with a preening motion. "Have you seen me?"

A genuinely truthful response would not have been very polite, so I fudged it a bit. "You certainly look familiar."

The brightness of her smile was about enough to make me go pitty-pat, pitty-pat. "How marvelous." She rattled off a list of credits, none of which struck any chords in my memory.

"I'm sure I must have seen you," I said, still damn well determined to be polite.

"I'm simply famished, Carl. Would you join me for a late supper?" By then she had already led me to the Patio Room, where not an hour before I'd had an onion-and-chopped-liver sandwich—no groaning allowed, they taste *good*—but by then I was also about 93.4 percent mesmerized by the china-blue depths of the eyes under those curling lashes. I'm not entirely sure I would have objected if she had said she wanted to pick my pocket. She was, after all, one *fine*-looking female. And I guess I'm as much a sucker for the attention of a beautiful woman as the next guy. I assured her I wouldn't mind a little bit.

"My treat," she insisted. "You did bring me such marvelous luck at that table."

I hadn't thought her luck was all *that* marvelous, but like I said, gamblers can be strange people at times. And who was I to quarrel with someone else's superstitions.

By the time she had eaten a third of a club sandwich—I'd settled for a sweet roll and coffee—I was wondering just how weird the gamblers got around here.

I mean, here was this really elegant creature right off the silver screen, and she was coming on with about as much subtlety as a mare in heat. Light, butterfly touches on the forearm and the inside of the wrist. Nudges of instep against ankle. Purrings accompanied by quick graspings above the knee. It was getting fairly steamy inside that open, airy restaurant, and I was finding it just a bit difficult to breathe. I practically expected her to come right out and ask if I'd do her the kindness of laying her.

She asked. Almost, anyhow. She leaned far forward, as if I hadn't already noticed the cut of her gown and that she wasn't wearing a bra under it, and said, "Isn't it odd, Carl, how winning always makes me feel, well," bat of the lashes, "quite horny, actually."

I gave serious consideration to imitating a coyote prowling under a full moon.

"Keno, sir?"

"What?" I was feeling downright disoriented. Coming back down to the real world took a moment.

Julie was standing beside the table with a sheaf of keno tickets and money in one hand and a chilly smile on her face. It was all I could do to keep myself from shaking my head to clear it.

"I asked if you would like to write a keno ticket, sir."

I smiled at her. Damn, she was cute. And sweet. And genuine. "I think I would at that, miss. Thank you." I turned my head a fraction so Sybil couldn't see and gave Julie a wink. It didn't seem to make any of the chill go away.

While Julie stood there I took one of the blank keno tickets from the supply available at every table in the place and used one of the always-available crayons to tick off the 9, 14, 42, and 77 squares. I gave the ticket and a buck to Julie.

"This is the way you fill them out, sir." With a strictly professional expression she showed me how to write in the amount of the bet and below that box the number 4 to show that that was how many squares I had marked.

"Thank you *very* much, miss." I hoped she would hear the rest of that message. But she didn't seem to be listening particularly well at the moment.

"Thank you, sir." She hurried off at the near trot that was her working pace.

I watched her go and was grateful for the interruption. That was one very nice girl. And I was in no condition for vigorous entertaining even if I was still in the mood. Which I wasn't.

"I was saying, dear . . ." Sybil began.

"Sorry. I guess I wasn't paying attention." I started to yawn, thought better of it as that might have been interpreted as an invitation, and said, "You know, Sybil, I really feel like this might be my night at the slots. Thanks for the snack." Before she might think up something even more direct, I gave her wrist a friendly squeeze, dropped a tip onto the table, and got the hell out of there.

I found Julie at the keno counter, waiting for the ticket

writers behind the long row of windows to validate her customers' tickets.

"Thanks," I said. "The cavalry arrived just in the nick of time to get me out of an embarrassing situation."

The look she gave me did not warm my heart. "You didn't look very embarrassed. Or like you needed saving." I thought I could see a little wetness brighten her eyes. "And it certainly wasn't very flattering to me that you'd have to turn to somebody like . . . *that!*"

"I didn't turn to anybody. And I was trying to avoid being picked up." Well, I could try to remember it that way, anyway. "And like what, anyhow?"

"You mean she hadn't gotten around to setting a price?" The pretty little Eurasian girl looked as prim as a New England spinster.

I was genuinely astounded. "She's a damn pro?"

I guess she could see that I was genuinely confused, which I damn sure was.

"You really didn't know." It wasn't particularly a question.

"Of course not. I was playing blackjack and the next thing I knew I was being draped with blonde."

One of the keno writers said something to her, and Julie turned away to collect her tickets.

"When will you get a break?" I asked.

She shrugged.

"Please. I have to talk to you." I pointed toward the lobby seating area where I had seen some of the keno runners take their breaks before. "Whenever it is, Julie, I'll be sitting up there waiting for you. Please."

She shrugged again, collected her tickets from the

window, and sorted through them until she found mine. She handed it to me. "Maybe," she said.

"I'll be there waiting."

The wait was not especially short, but that gave me some time to think while I sat.

I felt like a bit of a chump, actually. Carl Heller the ol' ladykiller. Knocks them over onto their backs with a single, suave glance. You bet.

Being with Julie was something else. It was as natural, and as good, as breathing.

But Sybil Stone was a pee-ure dazzler. If she really was a professional, she would have to be at least a five-hundred-dollar per-night bedmate. Maybe more. I'm not exactly expert on the going rates for top-flight call girls.

The point was—and she sure hadn't mentioned anything remotely resembling cash, nor am I quite fatheaded enough to think that a whore would be lusting for my body on a postman's holiday—if she had been sicced on me by somebody, that had to mean my friendly telephone contact had succeeded in putting out the word I wanted circulated.

And somebody wanted an inside source of information on a guy named Carl Heller. Very interesting, if true.

I sighed. The problem now was how to explain to Julie. I *liked* the girl. She sure didn't deserve any hurt feelings or sadness. She was just too nice a gal for that.

But as a reminder of what I was here for, and the kind of people I was dealing with, that little late-night snack with Miss Stone was quite effective.

I had to quit thinking about pretty ladies and blackjack tables and get down to business.

12

"I'd like to see Mr. Littori, please." I said it just as politely as I knew how, but I did add a crooked grin that could have been regarded as sarcastic.

The long-haired hippy creep looked like he didn't like me any better this visit than he had the last, but he seemed to have gotten some new orders since then. "Name?" he asked.

I deliberately misunderstood. "Littori. Anthony Littori."

He scowled and said, "His name I know, *sir.*" He bore down heavily on that last word, making it at least as sarcastic as my grin had been. "What is your name, *sir?*"

"Tell Mr. Littori that Carl Heller would like to talk with him." I smiled. Right pleasantly, I thought.

The creep left his stool—he had long since waved the girls away—and disappeared into the area marked for employees only. He was back in less than a minute. "This way."

I thought about digging him some about dropping the "sir" this time but thought better of it. The less I had to do with this kind of idiot, the better.

The more-or-less public areas of the Red Hat were plush in the extreme. The girls' rooms I had no idea about and cared less. The corridor the creep led me through was strictly utilitarian. Bare walls and tiled floor. No frills back here.

The office he showed me into was something else again.

If the parlor of this parlor house was what everyman's dream of an uptown bordello should be, then Tony Littori's office was that same schmuck's vision of what a corporate headquarters ought to look like. For some reason, it made me think Al Falcone's office would be very similar.

Dark, polished wood. Bookshelves with row after row of leather-bound spines showing. Draperied picture window overlooking a heart-shaped swimming pool, its concrete apron vacant at the moment. Overhead lighting recessed into the ceiling and hidden behind soffits or whatever the damn things are called. Couches, easy chairs, and massive, massive desk with its polished surface innocent of any annoying paperwork. I reminded myself that here they didn't work with paper in any event.

The man behind the desk was . . . average. About as average and ordinary-looking as any guy on any street. Average height and build, medium brown hair, features so normal he would be instantly forgettable in any gathering of two or more people. He wore a tan suit that looked like it came from a rack at Sears, pale blue shirt, and tan tie half a shade darker than the material of the suit. He stood when I came in, smiled in a perfectly ordinary manner, and offered his hand. I shook it and introduced myself.

"A pleasure, Mr. Heller. What can I do for you?"

"I thought it might be a nice idea if we were to get acquainted, Mr. Littori."

He held up a hand, palm forward, and with his other hand motioned me into a handsome, leather-upholstered easy chair. "Please. Call me Tony."

I smiled and sat. "If you'll call me Carl, Tony."

"Good. Very good." He sat in the huge chair behind his desk and tented his fingertips while he leaned back. The gesture reminded me of someone, but I couldn't at the moment think of who it would be. "Now, Carl, what is it I can do for you today?"

I pursed my lips and gave that some thought. Very slowly, picking my words with care, I said, "I would think there might be a possibility, Tony, that we could, uh, have interests in common. Mutually advantageous interests, so to speak. But, uh, quite frankly, Tony, I don't know that I would be completely comfortable discussing them in, uh, unknown surroundings."

Littori grinned. Apparently he was a man who appreciated caution. "I don't suppose it would help if I were to assure you that we are completely alone here."

"Not a whole lot, Tony, no."

"Of course." He sighed and swiveled around to look out the big window while he pondered the question of how we might be able to speak freely, without either of us bugging the other.

Beyond him, by the pool, a couple came into view. Very handsome pair, I thought. A thin, chocolate-colored girl with an Afro like a basketball and a middle-aged, lard-hipped man whose goosepimpled flesh was so pale he looked like a freshly plucked chicken. The girl shucked her bright orange Danskin and helped the man out of his skivvies, which was all he had been wearing. She tried to help him into the pool, too. Instead, he helped her onto her knees.

"Odd," I said into the silence of the office, "that no one seems to object to being looked at out there." What they were doing out there now was certainly something I wouldn't want watched by strangers. Or even awfully close friends.

"Reflective glass," Littori said. "From the outside it's made to look like a solar collector panel. If any of them ask, which they usually don't, the girls tell them that's what it is." He swiveled his chair back to face me and smiled. "Hell, they know they're being hustled anyway. That's what they come here for."

I gave him a grin and an appreciative chuckle. "That's the natural truth, Tony." I left my chair and stepped forward the few necessary paces to shake his hand again. "Damned if I don't like you, Littori."

Good old Tony tossed his head back and laughed. A happy man, Mr. Littori.

"Tell you what we could do, Carl. You and I could take a little drive. You know, go into town. Find a nice public restaurant or something. Neither your place nor mine, if you know what I mean."

"That sounds like a just-fine idea, Tony."

He leaned forward to touch a button on his intercom and call for his car to be brought around. A moment later we were on our way out of his office.

The poor rooster out by the pool would not have noticed us leave if we had posted signal flags. And the girl who was taking his money probably wouldn't have given a damn if the Salvation Army had been passing in review.

13

After we were on the road—in a Lincoln limo, but a plain old factory version instead of some wild custom like Falcone's—Littori suggested a nice public restaurant, and I said I didn't think so. Then I made a suggestion, which he declined. We compromised by finding a phone booth, opening the Yellow Pages to the proper section, and making a blind finger stab. Which took us to a Burger King on West Fourth. It was, I figured, pretty damn safe from electronic eavesdropping, and I guess Littori decided the same.

Over coffee and onion rings and bacon double cheese double whatevers we got better acquainted, danced around with each of us being vague and evasive until finally I decided to lay it out for him.

"Let me tell you something, Tony," I said, leaning forward and speaking a little lower, not that any of the kids in the place were paying any attention to us. "I like you personally, and the word I hear is that you're a guy that can be trusted. You know what I mean?"

Littori shrugged modestly. "The thing is, Carl, where'd you hear that word? About me being trusted."

I shook my head. "I told the man I wouldn't mention his name, so I guess I won't."

"It'd make a difference, Carl."

"Hell, I know how it is. Half the people you come in contact with are trying to set you up for something. Most of the other half would like to. What I want is a straightforward business deal. There's something I'd like to buy. It's just possible that you, uh, might know where I could make some purchases."

Littori managed to look innocent. I thought that was a helluva trick. "All I have to sell, Carl, are a few services out at the Red Hat Ranch."

"I've heard that, and I appreciate what you're saying," I told him with a grin. "Under the circumstances, Tony, what with us not knowing each other very well and all that, one of us is going to have to make a plunge, and I figure it's my place to be the one. So I'll lay it out straight for you and let you chew it over. Then we can talk or you can walk away or whatever. Okay?"

He nodded. He also looked thoughtful.

The story I gave him was a much-expanded version of the rumors I'd had Falcone's people plant in the seedier circles of Nevada.

I was a clean-on-paper old boy from the back woods of Colorado who didn't seem to do much but who kept coming up with chunks of unaccountable cash—which was true enough for a fact and a hassle at tax time every year—and now I was getting hungry. I was figuring to open a whorehouse, quite illegal in Colorado, by way of expensive "guest cabins" on the ranch I already owned there. I was in Reno, the rumor said, on a recruiting drive.

"It's an honorable profession in the mountains," I told him, "even if it isn't exactly within the letter of the law these days. Hell, Pearl deVere is just as well known in Cripple Creek as Julia Bullette was around here, and on up the line there's a legend about a girl called Silver Heels. Anyway, I figure nobody's going to bother me if I'm just renting out rooms at high prices and the company's thrown in for the mark to figure out by himself.''

Littori nodded. Like most hoods I've met, he had a liberal view on interpretations of the law. Well, so do I quite often, so I can't complain much about that.

"The thing is, Tony, with the ski areas out there I have a good clientele on tap, but there's freelancers and freebies everywhere you look. Snowbunnies willing to give it away for a flop and tomorrow's lift ticket. Like that. So if I want to do any good, I'll need to offer a, uh, specialized trade. If you know what I mean."

"Could be," he said.

"Very young for part of it, of course. Very, uh, vigorous for the rest. Extremely vigorous for some. So my turnover rate will be pretty high. I need a regular source of supply.

"What I figure to do is give the cabins small basements suitable for specialized facilities, the usual leather goods and such, and put them plenty far apart so there won't be any problem of sound carrying from one cabin to the next. I don't have a neighbor problem, and I have a few acres to work with, so I figure that's the way to go."

Littori smiled. "Four thousand two hundred and eleven acres," he said. "More or less."

I didn't have to pretend when I wanted to look surprised.

"I've been doing some homework," Littori admitted.

"Hell, I practically just hit town."

Littori shrugged. "You gave your name to my man at the door. The rest was just a matter of asking favors of friends." He paused. "The cops out there know about you. They don't all know what to make of you."

"If you know that," I told him, "you also know there's no convictions on my record."

"A few complaints. Some odd questions."

It was my turn to shrug. I knew what each and every one of those had been about, but if he wanted to read something else into them, which sure seemed likely, he was more than welcome to do so. In fact, I was almost counting on it.

"Some of those cops come on like friends of yours," he said.

"If I had to make a guess, Tony, I'd imagine that you have some friends around here too."

His grin was answer enough.

"Your civilian friends are a closemouthed bunch," he said.

"Ain't it nice to have friends," I said agreeably.

"Tell me more about the specialties you have in mind."

"Mostly very young stuff. They'll at least be reusable for quite a while. Anything bigger would have to go direct to the hard users. I'll set my prices on an escalating scale depending on, uh, damage. Disposal will be no problem on the, uh, premises, so to speak. Resupply is what I'm most worried about. I could pick up some down south. I have a few contacts there. But I couldn't count on them for the kind of demand I anticipate. I figure my projected turnover rate would be about five new units a month."

Littori nodded. He seemed to be thinking. He was also, I noticed, taking awfully calmly the idea that I planned to open a whorehouse specializing in child abuse and torture and figured to kill off about five girls a month doing it.

Jesus! Al Falcone's brief rundown on the way it is in the real, rotten world had seemed more than could be possible, back in the peace and security of my own living room.

Here, talking with one of the flesh peddlers who made that kind of thing possible, it looked like Falcone had given me an underplayed summary of it. And that son of a bitch Falcone had been offended only for fear that it might kill off his golden goose, too. The fact of it had not seemed to bother him at all.

Littori smiled. "New units," he said. "That's a very nice way to put it, Carl."

"Thank you."

"Naturally, I wouldn't know personally about anything like what you've been talking about."

"I wouldn't expect you to, Tony." We were talking for the record now, of course. "Besides, this entire idea has been a movie plot I've had in mind and just wanted to try out on someone. I expect you understood that right along."

Littori grinned. "I thought it was something like that, Carl." He shoved aside the paper litter from his meal and said, "I've really enjoyed meeting you, Carl. We should get together again sometime. Maybe, uh, tomorrow evening?"

"I'd like that, Tony. I damn sure would."

"Drop out to the place late tomorrow. Eleven or thereabouts?"

"That would be fine."

We smiled and shook hands and rode back to the Red Hat in the limo deep in conversation about the San Francisco Forty-Niners' recent draft choices. Littori thought they had made a few mistakes, and he had some firm opinions about exactly when and how those mistakes had happened. I agreed with practically every word the man said.

14

I'd been doing just fine sitting there with Littori, role-playing the part that was required if I was ever really going to learn anything about the man, being just as much of a scumbag as he was. It was a little while later that I began to think seriously about what I'd been doing, the kind of person I'd been representing myself to be.

Littori had dropped me off outside the Red Hat, and I'd removed the Vetterlite from the helmet lock on the side of the red Beemer. I took the gentle rollercoaster ride back on Interstate 80 toward Reno, past the other places, including Falcone's Falcon's Nest, which probably was just as unpleasant as the Red Hat.

About halfway back to the 395 interchange, with the Truckee River running darkly off to my left and the gaudy lights of Reno not yet in sight, the viciousness of it all hit me.

I felt a cold emptiness in my belly, and my arms were weak. Even that sweet-riding BMW was too much for me to handle at the moment, and I had to pull over to the side to park it and get off. I took off the helmet and sat with it between my knees, grateful for the solid feel of the concrete under me, drinking deep of the chill night air and hoping I would not puke and mess up one of the few pairs of slacks I had brought with me.

To pay a woman for the use of her body is one thing. To abuse a child's unwilling body and destroy her soul in the doing of it . . . that is a monstrous thing.

And the worst part of it was that for those few minutes I had been talking about it with Littori, I had been just as monstrous and evil as any of them.

Convincing him, or trying to, I had convinced myself, if only for those minutes.

I disgusted myself.

Because, however falsely, for whatever righteously self-important reasons, for those brief moments in time I had felt within myself a flickering spark of lust.

It seemed too glibly easy to say that the actor must play his role to the fullest. That I had to believe it if I expected to inspire belief. Easy and maybe even true.

But the thing that disgusted and frightened me was the thought that even in me I had discovered a capacity for titillation by something so utterly evil.

I wouldn't have believed that was possible.

I didn't *want* to believe it even now.

Simple curiosity? The thrill that comes with the breaking of a deep-rooted taboo? Perhaps no more than that.

The fact remained that if that faint ember could exist in me, I would have to presume it could exist in anyone. Fan that ember, encourage it, give it opportunity to flourish, and perhaps any of us could become as evil as Tony Littori and the men like him.

The thought made me shudder and feel a wave of nausea that threatened to relieve me of my Burger King meal.

"Dammit," I said aloud into the night. The trucks and

vacation-bound campers passing me on the interstate neither heard nor answered.

I sighed and lit a cigarette, absolutely unwilling at the moment to worry about things like surgeon general's reports or good advice from the Cancer Society. At the moment I was concerned about a form of cancer that was even worse, for no surgeon could ever cut this cancer away from society.

I smoked that smoke and flipped it away and lit another, sitting with my back to the highway and my eyes lifted to the brilliant spread of stars far overhead, and after a time I felt somewhat better.

Not all of us are lousy, by God. And none of us has to be.

For those few sons of bitches who encouraged this cancer there might not be surgeons who could heal them or undo their damage.

But, by the Lord God, there are some few of us who can use surgical steel to cut the source of the cancer away from society and keep it from infecting any more than have already been ruined.

I stood and brushed off my butt and buckled the Vetterlite back into place.

Piss on a bunch of regrets and self-examinations, I thought. There was something here that I might be able to *do* something about.

I damn sure figured to do it.

15

"I didn't see you last night."

"No, you didn't," Julie agreed.

"Look, I am truly sorry if I offended you. That was not my intention. As far as that woman was concerned, I didn't *have* any intentions. She was just another player in the casino as far as I knew. I had no idea. . . ." I shrugged. "I'm sorry. That's all it comes down to. I don't even know her. You, I like very, very much. I would like . . . quite desperately . . . to be able to hold you again." As I said it I realized that it was true. "If you don't want me to touch you, if you don't want any more than that, well, I can understand. You've been hurt, regardless of my intentions or lack of them. But . . . I would *really* like to be able to put my arms around someone decent and sweet and good, and just . . . hold you for a minute. If that wouldn't be too much to ask."

The more I talked to her the more I realized just how desperately I did want to touch and hold someone who was not evil and twisted. Someone normal and decent. Julie would have been ideal. A stranger would have done. It was human contact, not sex, that I craved right now. She might have heard something of that in my voice, or maybe she could see that I was on the thin edge of tears, ready to weep for the lost innocents too late for anyone to help. Maybe she heard or saw or simply sensed some of that.

Whatever the reason, her eyes softened and her lips parted from their firm, set line and she stepped closer to me to touch my arm.

She was on duty, supposed to be working, when I caught her in mid-rush, but she said, "I can tell them I'm coming down sick, Carl. Go up to your room. I'll . . . be along as soon as I can."

I felt my face twist and was barely able to bring it back under control. I felt too rocky to say anything at all at that moment, so I nodded a quick thank-you and bolted for the elevators before I went and embarrassed myself the way a grown man is never supposed to do.

"You really needed me, didn't you? I mean truly *needed* me."

"Yes." I wrapped her small, slim, marvelous, *clean* body closer against me and kissed her temple and her eyes and each perfect dimple.

"Do you want to talk about it?"

I sighed and shook my head. The temptation was great, but the risks were greater.

I knew good and well that Tony Littori had excellent contacts and quick sources of information. To tell Julie about any of this would give me a measure of relief, but it would burden her, and, worse, it could be a true disaster for some youngster neither she nor I would ever know. One word to the wrong person or one word overheard by the wrong stranger and Littori might know that his Colorado whoremaster was a hunter instead of a user.

"It isn't necessary," I told Julie. "You've already made

me whole again. Just being able to touch you and know you and hold you close, that's exactly what I needed."

She snuggled closer and her voice was joyful and tender when she said, "No one has ever needed me like that before, Carl. Never." She nuzzled my neck. "Thanks."

"I'm the one who has to thank you, believe me."

"Then it was special for both of us. I'm glad."

She closed her eyes and seemed to drowse a little, and I ran my hand across her shoulder and down over the firm, ripe rise of her breast to the flat perfection of her belly.

Her body was small. It could be called childlike in its size. Yet with her there was no taint of the taboos against the child lovers. She was a woman. More, she gave herself freely and happily and with delight in her ability to impart pleasure and to receive it.

Most important of all, when I was with her I was with *her*. Not with a body to be used but with a *person*. With skin as with books, it is what is *inside* that is important. The outside is only so much window dressing.

"Do you have any idea," I whispered, "what a good and a valuable person you are, Julie Jones?"

She smiled and clung to me with a fierceness I had not expected, but I welcomed it and found myself returning it in kind.

That cheerful, sensitive, willingly giving girl held me and healed me and wiped away my doubts and my hurts, and I will be grateful to her forever.

It was very late before we slept, and when we did it was the being with her that left me more refreshed than any amount of sleep could have done.

16

Littori met me at the door himself, smiling and confident and relaxed. I took it that this was a mark of favor from the way the slack-faced whores were cutting sideways glances in our direction.

The place was busy at this time of evening, the main room full of the sounds of conversation from the bar and only a few, eight or ten, of the girls available for the lineup. Littori looked the scene over with obvious satisfaction and gave the whores the benediction of his smile. Two or three of them even smiled back. The man was a real charmer.

"Come in, Carl." He took me by the elbow to keep me from heading back toward his office. "Better yet, it's such a nice evening, why don't you and I walk down by the river. I'd enjoy that."

I gave him a phony smile. "Good idea." Good idea indeed. Inside the Red Hat he could and almost certainly did have an ample supply of bugs on hand to eavesdrop on every niche and corner. Anywhere I might choose to go, he could have planted some gadgets. The open riverbank could be presumed to be neutral territory.

Littori led the way, some unseen hand pushing the electric buzzer to open the gate and let us pass through.

In spite of the daytime heat in this high-desert country,

the evenings carried a chill that was a welcome reminder of
the fresh, clean, high-country air I was used to at home. It
felt good.

The Truckee ran not a hundred yards from the front gate
of the Red Hat, swift and full at this time of year with the
runoff snowmelt from the Sierras off to the west. The
riverbed here was relatively smooth and the water ran
without obstruction or burbling chatter. Not good rafting
potential by any means, which was a shame. Swift water
without chutes or rocks always seems like a waste of
opportunity to me.

Littori picked his way through the lush streamside grass
and I trailed along behind, conscious of the bright starlight
that illuminated the scene. I will admit it crossed my mind
that the whoremaster and I could not be seen from the Red
Hat's watchtower unless the guard up there had a starlight
scope to keep us in view. One quick, soundless flurry of
motion, and Anthony Littori could find himself taking a
deep, miles-long bath in the cold waters of the Truckee
River. That would solve a lot of problems for a lot of
people.

I sighed. Having to think of myself as a murderer would
put an awful crimp in my opinion of myself. And besides, if
Littori disappeared—aside from the fact that his hirelings
back inside the Red Hat knew whom he was walking out
with—there might well be someone else around who would
be willing and able to pick up the business where the boss
left off.

Littori stopped. "Does this look all right?"

"Over here might be better." I led the way this time, not
farther in the direction he had been going but back upstream
a ways. I smiled at him. "Just in case, you understand."

Littori laughed. "You're all right, Carl. I *like* you." I've received compliments that thrilled me more, like from people I had some respect for. Still, this wasn't the time to be thinking about that.

"Good. I like you too, Tony. And I think maybe we understand each other."

"I think we do at that."

He was wearing another off-the-rack suit but a pretty nice one. He didn't let that bother him any, just picked out a reasonably soft-looking spot and sat on the grassy slope. I sat beside him.

We sat in silence for a few minutes, smoking and watching the pinpricks of light wheel slowly overhead, then Littori said, "Those, uh, commercial units we were talking about before, Carl?"

"Uh-huh."

"I might be able to help you."

I crushed out my cigarette in the dark earth at my side. "I'm glad to hear that, Tony."

"I did a little more checking on you. I hear you don't talk much, and people don't talk much about you."

"It's a useful way to have it," I agreed.

"They say your word is good."

"That's even more useful."

Littori sat doing some thinking for a moment. "Ten thousand per unit," he said. "It isn't a negotiable price. Yes or no."

"Practically everything is negotiable," I said. I was afraid if I rolled over too easy on the first price he set, he might get the idea that I was some kind of cop setting him up with funds out of the public till.

"Not this," Littori said.

"Considering the reorder volume I have in mind," I told him, "I think this ought to be."

He thought that over for a minute or two. "I might be willing to negotiate the figure when it comes time to work out a resupply schedule. The initial stocking would have to be at that level."

It was my turn to sit and think it over. Business is business after all, whatever the commodity. Right, Tony? Creep! I sat and smoked another one and pretended to mull it over.

"I'll need a sample," I said. "I don't intend to commit myself on the basis of blind faith."

"I have a few, uh, units you can choose from."

I nodded. "Payment on delivery."

"How soon?"

"Tomorrow would be all right. I don't have the cash with me tonight."

Littori frowned. "I thought you weren't set up for business yet."

I stood, brushed off the seat of my britches, and flipped my cigarette toward the glossy black flow of the river. It spun in a bright red arc and extinguished itself in the water. "If you're asking what I intend to do with the sample, Mr. Littori, maybe I'd better run down to Mexico after all."

"Wait a minute, Carl. You don't have to be that touchy."

"On the contrary, Tony, we *both* have to be at least that touchy."

"I apologize. All right? Tomorrow night would be just fine with me, but I only have a small selection. Advance notice will let me do better. Is that all right with you?"

I nodded.

"It would be better if you don't come out here again. I'll send a car for you. Nine-fifteen at the shuttle stop. That's the south entrance. You'll recognize the driver."

I didn't express any surprise that he knew where I was staying. That only stood to reason. I nodded.

Littori stood and offered his hand. I shook it instead of spitting in his face or maybe breaking that face. Either would have been preferable to a handshake. The man had just agreed to sell me a human being.

He walked me back to the Beemer and waited while I pulled on helmet and gloves. "Tomorrow night," he said.

"Nine-fifteen," I agreed.

At least I didn't feel quite so rotten this time driving back to Reno. I left the visor of the helmet up to give me as much fresh air as possible and gave the RS one helluva wring-out. It seemed to help. It was even better that Julie was there waiting for me when I got back to the room.

17

"Ten thousand," I told the voice on the telephone. "Don't try to get cute, please. No markings or anything like that."

"You been watching too much TV," the voice said. "Nobody does it that way anymore. What the cops do, they Xerox the bills when they're fixing to make a buy. Much handier that way. Me, I don't give a shit if you're going t(

use the stuff for toilet paper. I'm told to help you, I'll help you. You'll get the money you want."

"How?"

"Don't sweat about it. You'll get it, okay?"

I would have asked him something more, but the line went dead as he hung up. A very chatty fellow, my helpful contact with Falcone and his sleazy pals. Still, it was the middle of the night, and not everyone would be on gamblers' hours, even in Reno.

I heard the water quit in the shower and smiled with anticipation. A moment later I was rewarded with the sight I had been hoping for. Julie came out of the bathroom with one towel wrapped turbanlike around her head and another trailing from her hand. It wasn't hiding very much. Her small body was a study in golden-cream perfection.

"How'd you know I'd want to hold you close tonight?" I asked her. She had called in sick so she could be with me when she should have been working her keno shift.

"What makes you think it wasn't me wanting to be with you and that magic tongue of yours?" She gave me a grin and began crawling across the expanse of bed that separated us. Both towels managed to get left behind in the process.

"If *that*'s all you want, it makes me think you don't respect me." I tried to get up, but she leaped the last few feet and pounced on me with exquisitely accurate aim. "On the other hand . . ." I murmured.

For such a little girl there seemed to be an awful lot of her at times, and she sure was a nimble and busy little thing. It was quite a while before I thought about anything except Miss Jones.

                              * * *

Breakfast alone is not something I would deliberately choose when there is another option available, but Julie hadn't wanted to be seen by any of the staff, including the room-service waiters. Besides, she said, she wanted to change her clothes. So she went home and I waited a decent interval before I took the elevator down to the casino level for a solitary, ninety-nine-cent breakfast in the Stage Door Cafeteria.

I ate quickly, decided the scenery would be better in the casino than in the cafeteria, and ambled out that way.

As I reached the exit, a grinning little man with thinning hair and bifocals stepped in front of me. He looked like a typical tourist in shorts and sandals and a Hawaiian print shirt. All he lacked was a camera slung around his neck.

"Ed," he said happily, right into my face. "Ed Sherman. Damn. Fancy meeting you here." He grabbed my hand and pumped it. "Oh!" His eyes went wide, and his face became blood red with embarrassment. "You aren't Ed. S-sorry," he stammered. He backed away, looking considerably flustered, and fled. He was there and gone in seconds.

He also left behind a metallic something in the palm of my hand.

Very, very nice, I thought. If I hadn't been able to feel whatever it was he had passed, I would have bought the performance myself. I stuffed both hands into my pockets and wandered away in search of a restroom where I could examine the thing.

It turned out to be a safety-deposit-box key with the MGM logo on it. When I found the appropriate desk and presented the thing, everything was in order. A few minutes later the unsuspecting clerk swapped my key for a thick, legal-sized envelope that had my name and room number typed on it.

I wasn't particularly amazed to discover that the envelope held ten thousand cash, in fifty- and hundred-dollar bills.

Efficient, I thought. Both Falcone and Littori seemed to be almighty efficient.

I began to wonder if maybe this time I was playing outside my rustic, backwoods league. A cowboy butting heads with the professionals. That could, I reflected, be a good way to get one's skull broken.

18

I did indeed recognize the driver. He was the long-haired hippy creep who was usually on duty at the door of the Red Hat. This evening he was in the driver's bucket of a jazzy little white LN7. The California tag with the digit 1 at the front said it was a rental. It also turned out to be an underpowered pup with a transmission that made its ride rougher than some broncs I've ridden. Whiplash seemed imminent. And my concentration was on the car and the route. The driver was not interested in conversation.

He took me north and east, staying off the four-lane throughways, finally finding a state or county road that meandered off into the rugged, semimountainous desert terrain. We rode in silence like that for the better part of an hour before he pulled off the pavement onto a dry dirt track and drove another half-hour or so on that.

Eventually we came to a stop behind the dark bulk of a van that was blocking the way.

"Up there," the long-hair said. As far as I could recall, they were the first words he had spoken since he had picked me up.

The van door opened on the passenger side as I approached, and the interior light came on. Tony Littori stepped out to meet me. He was smiling.

"Evening, Carl." We shook and exchanged a few pleasantries.

He led me away from the van a few paces and asked, "I hope you won't mind if we make sure you aren't wired."

"Not at all."

Littori motioned, and a middling-sized creep with short hair came out of the driver's side of the van to give me a thoroughly professional pat down that included all the private places where recorders or transmitters might be hidden. At close range, Littori's bodyguard—an assumption, of course—wasn't much for size, but he carried himself with the agile efficiency of an athlete.

"Nothing but a pistol, Mr. Littori," he said after he had examined the contents of my pockets and even checked the magazine of my Smith to make sure there was nothing in there but 9mm cartridges. The fact that I was carrying seemed perfectly acceptable to both of them.

"Thank you, Leo."

Leo nodded and went back to the van.

Littori motioned me over to the side of the van and slid back the cargo door. Without being asked, Leo snapped on an overhead light.

The inside of the vehicle was probably twenty-five thousand dollars' worth of plush, but what caught my attention were the passengers.

There were two girls in there. Or, more accurately, one girl and a young woman. Littori gave me time to look them over.

The one on the left of the crushed-velvet couch in the back of the van was probably eighteen or nineteen years old and outwardly pretty in a thin, pale, lifeless sort of way. Her eyes were as dull as her hair, and she was staring off toward some dim, distant place without any apparent interest in her surroundings. I got the impression I would not want to know what the past few years had been like for her. Her skin looked as dry and as fragile as parchment. She never glanced in my direction while I was inspecting her.

The other girl could not have been more than fifteen years old, I thought. She obviously wasn't into grooming or personal hygiene as her thing, but her figure was ripe.

She wore cutoff jeans short enough for the pockets to hang out below the denim fabric, and a halter top that showed melon-sized breasts somehow still firm and full with the tautness of youth. Her nipples were a pinky-thick statement that she did not give a damn about the opinions of her elders. Her hair was a long tangle of medium blond mane that would have been an asset if she'd bothered to brush it. Unlike the older girl, all the flesh I could see—and there was a good bit of it—was deeply tanned and tight. Her facial features were rather plain, but her youth made up for it, giving her a look of ersatz innocence that seemed odd under the circumstances. She gave me a bold look and a wink while I was looking at her.

Littori let me look them over as much as I wanted, which

didn't take very long, and when I turned away he led me out away from the van. The going was rocky underfoot and both of us stumbled and muttered our way seventy-five yards or so into the dark desert.

"Well?"

"The young blonde," I said. The older one looked like she had already been through the wringer. If I could spring only one of them, it should be the one who looked like there could still be some promise there.

"I thought you'd like her," Littori said. He managed to make it sound quite nasty indeed. "They were told you're recruiting for a massage parlor. You won't have any trouble with either of them if you stay with that."

"All right." I paused to light a smoke. "Assuming I like the sample, and I can't see any reason not to, how young can you go, Tony?"

He shrugged. "It varies. Fourteen to sixteen is normal. Not usually under twelve. I can get you some twelves to fourteens if you want them." He sounded as matter-of-fact as if he were discussing dress sizes instead of ages.

And he'd told them that they were going into a massage parlor, obviously an illegal one. They'd accepted that as everyday stuff, apparently, even the young one. Jesus, I'd been leading a sheltered life up until now.

"No chance they could have told anyone where they might be headed?" I asked, thinking it the sort of question my role demanded.

"No way," Littori assured me. "What you let yours do after you take delivery, of course, is up to you. As a rule, they don't want to communicate with anybody back home. Later on it will be too late, if you know what you're doing."

I nodded. Sure. Easy. Once they were used up, it would

be entirely too late. He expected them to be dead by then. I managed to suppress a shudder.

I pulled the wad of Al Falcone's cash out of my pocket and handed it to Littori. "I think we're going to get along just fine for a long time to come, Tony."

He smiled and put the money into his pocket without counting it. I guess he figured I wouldn't try to stiff him on a sample purchase when there was more business to be done later.

We walked back to the van and Littori said, "You could do me a big favor if you would, Carl."

"Of course, Tony."

"You could take Linda home for me. It would be a big help. Just leave the keys to the little car under the mat and park it at your hotel. Would you do that?"

I smiled my appreciation of his wording. Nothing had been said that would be remotely incriminating if every federal agent in Nevada had it on tape.

"I'd be happy to, Tony."

"Linda." He motioned the blond girl out of the van. "Honey, this is my friend Carl. He'll take you wherever you want to go."

She retrieved a small purse from inside the van and stood in front of me looking me over, very much the same way I had so recently inspected her. It felt kind of odd being looked at that way. After a moment she grunted and nodded.

The older girl still had not responded to anything that was said or done around her.

Linda was shorter than I had realized, not much taller than Julie although much fuller of figure. She looked me over with a cocky insolence, tilted her head, and said,

"Anytime you're ready." Her voice was much younger than her body.

She certainly seemed to be traveling light. Two ragged garments and a clutch purse. That seemed to be all she needed. She went and got into the LN7, and the long-haired hippy creep got out, leaving the door open for me.

"Go straight back that way to the blacktop," he said, "and turn left. You can't miss all those lights."

I said my thanks and my good-byes to Littori, assured him for the record that I would take good care of his "guest" and see her safely to wherever she wanted to go, and got the hell out of there.

"Tell me about this place where we're—"

"Later," I cut the girl off. "We'll talk when we're out of this car."

No questions, no argument. She shut her mouth and didn't open it again on the long drive back to town.

I was glad. I was having enough trouble trying to adjust to the idea that I had just purchased a person without having to carry on a conversation with her too.

"Jesus!"

It wasn't an exclamation; it was a prayer.

19

There was this one tiny little detail that I hadn't exactly thought out in advance. Or thought of at all, for that matter.

Now that I had the girl, what the hell did I do with her?

My impression of the MGM Grand was that they would frown on lecherous old SOBs who wanted to take fifteen-year-old girls to their rooms, and I was long since checked in as a single. It was a bit late to think of a father-daughter pose or some such.

And I was a thousand miles from home and the kind of help I could find there. Like privacy for conversations and a whole lot more information about Tony Littori and his promises. I really needed to get her back there. Somehow. I sighed. The BMW seemed to be the only logical way to do it.

I parked the car on the outer fringes of the nightly casino crowd, left the keys as instructed, debated whether I should lock the car when I left it, and finally decided not to bother. The rental car was Littori's problem.

"We're going for a ride," I told the girl as we crossed the asphalt toward the lot where I had left the Beemer.

"Yeah?" She sounded somewhat less than thrilled, bored if anything. It seemed a strange attitude. She was still just a kid and seemed to own nothing in the world but a couple scraps of cloth and whatever she carried in that little purse; and she had been told she was going to be employed as a massage-parlor hooker, yet she came along as tame as a Jersey heifer without a question out of her mouth. I couldn't understand that.

It occurred to me about then, too, that I was persistently thinking of her as "the girl." Littori had called her Linda. Real name or fictional, I should have been thinking of her by name. I found that I didn't really want to. "The girl" was somehow more comfortable. Anthony Littori, I decided, was in one sordid son of a bitch of a business.

"How old are you, girl?"

She didn't look at me, just kept striding, trying to meet my pace. "Tony said you'd get me ID showing I'm old enough."

"I know that already. I asked how old you are."

"Seventeen."

"Bullshit." Maybe I shouldn't have used that kind of language, but that was what came out. Certainly it didn't seem to offend or shock her.

She shrugged. "Maybe a little less."

Great. I needed information, and what I had here, bought and paid for, was a regular little fount of it. A real chatterbox ready to spill out anything I wanted to know. You bet.

I could imagine how Littori—or Falcone, for that matter—would have handled it. They would have popped her one in the chops and quietly asked the question again. Not entirely my style, role-playing or not. I decided to ignore it.

We got to the BMW, and I discovered another unanticipated problem. When I'm traveling alone I only carry one crash helmet. As usual, the Vetterlite was locked to the side of the bike. One helmet short of enough, and for the life of me I couldn't remember whether either Nevada or Utah has a helmet law. In Colorado I can ride legally without one, although I don't. I tend to value my skull enough without having some legislature mandate the protection. But in the other states we would have to cross, there might well be laws requiring helmets. I thought I could do without a highway patrolman's questions on this trip.

Still, the choices were to go now or to find a place to stay overnight with this underaged bundle of tanned flesh. I didn't want to create a problem there. Not that I wanted the kid's bod; I just didn't want her wondering why the bossman wasn't taking a free sample. I didn't want her getting any kind of upset until we reached home.

I handed her the helmet, helped her strap it on, and figured I would just have to take my chances with the cops until I could find a place to buy another.

All of my luggage and riding gear were inside the brightly illuminated hotel just a hundred yards away, but I didn't want to take a chance on either taking her in there with me—it'd be a helluva thing to try to explain to Julie, for one thing—or leaving her alone while I went inside. The gear would just have to wait until I got back.

I fired up the Beemer and motioned for the girl to climb on behind me. She did it without a word, neither pleased nor annoyed at the prospect. That, too, was kind of unusual. Most people react fairly strongly to two-wheeled transportation, one direction or the other. This kid did not.

"Just sit there," I told her. "Don't lean with me or against me when I lay the bike over. If you sit upright in relation to the bike we'll be just fine." She didn't answer, so I just assumed that she had heard and understood.

I found an all-night gas station—no point in pretending any longer that they are service stations; all of those seem to have disappeared—and filled the bike before we headed into the wilderness. You can generally find gas along an interstate route, but in Nevada and Utah I wouldn't even count on that at night. For sure I wasn't going back by the empty US 50 route, not with long-haul night riding to do.

After I paid for the fuel—pocket change in spite of the current gas prices when you're filling a bike—I kept one eye on the girl through the plate-glass window while I placed a couple telephone calls. One to the MGM asking them to hold my room and not throw my stuff away. The other to Julie with some outright lies explaining my absence. She was sorry I had to be away for a few days. Personally, I was even sorrier.

"Ready?" I asked when I got back to the pump apron. The girl shrugged.

The kid was a real joy to travel with, I thought while I straddled the machine and thumbed the starter. And, dammit, I felt plumb naked without a helmet. I clicked the RS into gear and swooped back up onto I-80, blessing the man who had invented quartz halogen headlights *and* the guy who had come up with the crash helmet.

20

At mid-afternoon the next day I damn near killed the both of us. My excuse is that I was wiped out from too much road and too little sleep, my buns were numb from so many hours in the saddle, and my eyes were propped open but they just plain weren't registering much that went on in front of them.

I came whipping up behind a family of flatland tourists in a scabby green Toyota with Kansas plates, came up on them at something close to twice their speed, leaned on the left bar to swoop around them, and discovered that there was already a pickup truck occupying the lane. I came fully awake for the first time in probably more than an hour.

"Lordy," I mouthed, and clamped on both sets of binders hard enough to set up a wobble at the back tire and seriously reduce the amount of wear I could expect from this set of Continentals.

A kid in the backseat of the Toyota was staring out with his mouth gaping when I tucked in close enough to his daddy's rear fender that I could have touched it, and the pickup swished past with the driver's mouth beginning to drop open in a yell of anger that I was fairly sure I did not want to hear.

I was awake now for sure, hyped up on a rush of adrenaline that had my heart trying to beat its way out of my chest. I came off the brakes and off the throttle too and let the Beemer drift to a stop along the side of the road. The bike was too pretty to deserve being a hood ornament.

"We're going to stop here awhile," I told the girl. "I got to flake out for a few hours or we won't make it in intact."

She shrugged, got off, and began to unbuckle the el cheapo helmet I had picked up for her as soon as the stores had opened back in Utah. So far she had been anything but a problem. She sat there as placid as a cow, munched junk food and drank pop when we stopped for gas, and didn't even demand potty stops along the way. So far, being with her was much like hauling a dressmaker's dummy strapped onto the backseat.

And I couldn't complain either about the time we were making. I'd left the interstate back east of Salt Lake. Now we were on US 40 somewhere near Craig, Colorado, within one more fill-up of home. The only bad thing about that was that down off the superslab, the road and the riding were a hell of a lot more demanding than the autopilot, sleepytime reactions you could allow yourself on the gentle interstate highway. And I was just in no shape to ride the whipsaw switchbacks that were up ahead near Steamboat and Winter Park.

I got off the BMW and dragged it up onto the center stand—much as I love the breed, their kickstands were designed by a jibbering idjit—with nowhere near the easy motion that usually gets that job done.

"I'm all in, kid. We'll stretch out in the shade over there. If you wake up before I do, don't go wandering off anywhere. I don't want to lose you."

She nodded and followed me to a shortgrass slope above

the road cut where there was some scant shade provided by a stunty pine of some flavor. She didn't look a bit the worse for the wear and was still clutching that little purse of hers. She'd insisted on holding it in her hands the entire trip, even though I had offered to bungee it to the little carryall rack behind the backrest.

I lay down and motioned her down beside me. Here in the open, I figured, there was no likelihood that that would be interpreted as an invitation for her to audition.

The girl sat and began to rummage in her purse.

Shee-double-damn-it, I thought. She brought out a Baggie containing a rainbow assortment of pills, reached in to select one, and popped the thing into her mouth.

"What are you taking?"

She shrugged. "Stuff, man. Want some?"

I think I growled a little, but I'm not sure about that. I am sure that her eyes narrowed, and she got a suspicious and watchful expression on her face that made her look far older and far harder than her years gave her any right to be.

I thought about snatching the crap away from her and pitching them. I wanted to. But that would only have created a problem. I still had to get her back home, and I sure had to have her cooperation to do it. If I snatched her candy now, she would likely run off to find some more, and then where would I be? Call the cops to look for her? You bet. Officer, I bought an' paid for this teenage hooker and now she's run off and would you please fetch her back for me. Sure.

"No thanks," I told her. I sighed. At least that, or something, was keeping her content while I hauled her off into bondage.

Lordy, what an ugly world we do live in.

I closed my eyes and tried to pretend that her Baggie did not exist. And that people like Anthony Littori did not exist. And that everything was just the way it ought to be.

Pity it wasn't so.

After a little while I was able to sleep.

21

It took some time and a considerable amount of pounding before a light came on in the other end of the house. A minute later Walter opened up. He was wearing a robe that looked even older than he was. His white hair was tousled, and he was scowling. He looked ready to repel boarders— or at the least to chase away lost campers. His expression lightened when he saw who it was.

"Come in." He stepped back and held the door wide. I am reasonably sure it did not escape his notice that the girl with me was in her mid-teens.

"This is Walter," I told the girl. "You'll be seeing a lot of him."

She mistook my meaning and gave him a wink. Walter looks grandfatherly and is as good a neighbor and friend as a man could have, but I don't think he has much use for children until they are old enough to be people. He frowned at her and motioned her to a chair in the living room.

"The kid is Linda," I told him. "She'll be working for us."

"Right." He hadn't the foggiest notion what tale she might have been told, but he was willing to go along with it.

"Sit down, girl, we want to talk to you," I said.

"It's late, man. Time to crash."

"Nope. Time to talk. Just do what you're told and you'll be all right."

She made a face but seemed to resign herself to obedience.

"Do you want a drink, Carl?"

"A little sipping whiskey would be nice after the ride we've had," I told him.

"Two," the girl said.

"Right," Walter agreed. "One for Carl and one for me. Would you like a cola?"

"I want a drink, man. Something hard an' fiery."

"Suit yourself." Walter went into the kitchen. When he came back he had two glasses, one for me and one for himself. The girl got nothing.

Linda—I was beginning to be able to think of her by name now that I had her safely in surroundings where I could control things better—gave Walter a glare that would have withered most males and dug into her purse for the Baggie of pills. I went over and took away the purse. "Sorry, not here."

"Look, man, I . . ." She never finished whatever vulgarities she intended to enlighten us with. Mild-mannered old Walter turned out to have some strong and unsuspected opinions on the subject of drugs.

Before I realized what he was up to, he was at my side and had snatched the Baggie away from me. He shook it under her nose, and if her look had been withering, his was deadly. "Don't you ever, *ever* bring any of this shit where I can see it. Do you understand me?"

"Look, man, I . . ."

"Do you understand me?"

She nodded.

Walter took the Baggie and stomped out of the room. I could hear a toilet flush a moment later. So much for Miss Linda's stash of chemically induced rainbows. When he came back, Walter was puffing as if from a half-mile uphill run. He really looked pissed. "Don't you ever," he repeated.

Linda looked from him to me and back again several times. "What is it with you two, anyhow? I been promised work, man. You better deliver. An' what are you, queer? All this time and you haven't even wanted to be blown. How d'you know I'm any good?"

"You have experience, don't you?" I asked.

"Hell yes I got experience," she said. "Des Moines, Seattle, lately Frisco. You better believe I got experience."

"How'd you get connected with Tony?"

She shrugged. "A friend turned me on to 'im. Hell, you get tired of giving it away for a lousy toke or a place to crash, you know. This sounds like a good deal." Her eyes narrowed. "What the hell *is* this, anyhow? You old bastards aren't acting right at all."

Walter might've been used to it, I wouldn't know, but I'm not exactly used to being called an *old* bastard. Other adjectives, sure, but not that one. Perspective, I guess. But it did get my attention.

"Do you know what Tony got for passing you along to me?" I asked.

The shrug again. "A finder's fee. I don't care what it was, man. Just so I get my share of the play. You know?"

I shook my head. Couldn't help it. "Walter, to bring you up-to-date, I bought and paid for this kid here. What are you, fifteen?"

A shrug.

"She was told she'd be working in a massage parlor and that I could fix her up with ID to give her a legal age. Also that she'd be paid well for her services. What were you told those services would be, Linda?"

The shrug. "Same old jazz. Get the jerk's rocks off, whatever it takes. So what's the big deal?"

"So the big deal, girl, is that you've been sold down the river. Every way possible. You're nonreturnable merchandise, girl. As far as good old Tony knows, I'm running a whorehouse out here. A specialty shop."

"So?"

"So one of the specialties these boys like to dabble in is torturing young girls like you. Whips and knives and the whole bad scene."

"I don't go for that shit, man. I'll screw anything that's got balls, but I don't go the S-and-M scene. You'd better know that."

"Listen to me, dammit. If you'd gone to another buyer, you'd do *any*thing you were told to do, and it wouldn't be over until you were dead. Do you understand what I'm trying to tell you, Linda? You're meat on the hoof to those bastards. They don't care what happens to you once they have their money."

"Bullshit," she said with girlish gentility. Uh-huh.

"What do you think a pimp would pay ten thousand bucks for, Linda? Another average hooker? No way."

"Bullshit."

"Linda," Walter said, "whether you choose to believe us or not, the facts are exactly as Carl has explained them to you."

"And now we need to know everything you can tell us about Tony and all his friends."

"No fuckin' way, man. I don't know what you jerks are up to, but I'm leaving." She got up and would have headed for the door, but Walter grabbed her by the arm. The old boy wasn't particularly gentle about it, either. "Sit," he snarled. She sat.

"We aren't asking you, Linda. We're telling you," I said. "You are going to tell us everything you know or so much as suspect about Tony Littori and his friends."

"Bullshit," she said again, but this time she sounded frightened.

Terrorizing a child is hardly a thing to give a man cause for pride and satisfaction. But at least, I thought, if she could be frightened verbally we might get some help out of her after all. We damn sure couldn't beat her into submission, so maybe her fear was of benefit. I tried to rationalize it that way, anyhow, and said and did nothing to make the child feel any better about us.

In the end she vowed, loudly and with fairly inventive language for a youngster, that she would get the hell away from us old bastards and tell Tony straightaway that there were some weirdos on his tail. We really needed that.

"I don't see that we have a helluva lot of choice," I told Walter hours later when I thought we had extracted about all the useful information from her that we could hope for. "We have to keep her under wraps until Tony has taken his fall.

We can't let her loose or she'll run straight back to the son of a bitch."

"We could take her to the police, Carl."

"Walter, I'm real proud to see that a man of your age can still retain a childlike faith in the purity of the guys who wear white hats. But there are a couple things that say that isn't possible. Apart and aside from the fact that what I did myself over in Nevada was highly illegal.

"For one thing, both that girl and Littori would lie about our sad story. It would be my word against theirs, and without a victim there's no way the cops would believe us.

"For another, Littori has as much as admitted to me that he owns a few boys in blue. He thinks I do too. We don't know how many or which ones, but even if we did, they could tip him before any straight cop could get a judge to do anything. They have to worry about warrants and crap like that, you know.

"So what I think we have to do is to keep Little Miss Sunshine wrapped up here while I go back to Reno and find a way to use this stuff about Littori's little playpen of underage kids. Can you do it?"

Walter sighed. He looked tired. "I can do it, Carl."

With the girl listening, we talked it over and decided finally on my basement as the best place to keep her. There wasn't anything down there hardly, except for my weight machine, and if she was strong enough to wreck that, we couldn't hold her in a gorilla cage anyhow. Walter would move his stuff into my house until I got back, and the girl would live—if not happily, then at least breathing, which was better than what she'd been slated for—in my cellar until I could get home again. Then we could turn her loose with a bus ticket and some advice that she call her parents. I couldn't at the moment think of anything better than that for her. As near as I could tell, there was not a hell of a lot of hope we could hold out for this one. I just hoped we could do more for some others that Tony didn't have yet.

22

The ride back to Reno was tiring but not nearly as hectic as that eastbound leg had been. I took two full days to do it and called Julie from a good many miles out so she could be waiting for me when I got there. To say it was a pleasure to see and to hold someone gentle and nice and normal, well, that would have been an understatement without parallel. I think she sensed some of that.

"Are you all right, Carl?" she asked when she was done with a thoroughly accomplished hello kiss.

"Now I am."

She tucked in close against my chest, and I could feel the warmth of her breath through the material of my shirt.

"Do you have to work tonight?"

"I'm afraid so," she said. She gave me an elfin grin. "Everyone is glad that I'm feeling better. I wouldn't want them to worry about a relapse."

"Okay." I kissed the glossy, sweet-scented hair on top of her head and stroked her cheek. I wanted to ask her to stay the night, but I couldn't. She had work to do, and there was no way I was going to offer to compensate her for the lost pay if she stayed. Other times and other places I might have and not thought a thing about it. Not here. Not now.

"We still have almost six hours before I have to report in," she said. She grinned up at me and gave me a parody of a bawdy wink.

"If I'd thought of that," I said, "I'd have collected a pocketful of speeding tickets getting here. And every one of them would have been worthwhile."

Julie slipped out of my arms and closed the drapes in my cleaned but apparently undisturbed room. With all the naturalness and sweetness in the world she stood in the dim half-light and undressed. When she came to me she was a joyous cleansing for a bruised and battered soul, and I was grateful that she was there.

She fumbled at the unfamiliar task of taking a cigarette from the pack and stuffed it a half-inch too deep between my lips, then bent quite seriously to the chore of scratching a match alight and holding it for me. When the smoke was lit she found an ashtray and balanced it on my belly. I was still breathing a bit heavily, and she giggled at the way that made the ashtray bounce and wobble. I stroked the ivory perfection that was her back.

"You're definitely a nice person, Julie Jones. I think I like you."

"Huh. You'd better do better than that if you want seconds, buster."

"Seconds? Did I lose count somewhere? Imagine things that didn't happen?"

"In polite company, anything after the first is considered to be seconds."

"Yes, ma'am. In that case, I will admit that I *definitely* like you. Better?"

"Better," she agreed. She gave up her ashtray watching and snuggled down against my shoulder. After a few seconds she raised up on her elbow and looked me in the eye. "I hope I'm the only one you like in this hotel." She sounded serious.

"Not to worry, pretty lady. You are the one and only captor of my heart right now. And other things too if it matters."

"It does," she said. She started to speak, then closed her mouth.

"What?"

"Nothing."

"That tone of voice doesn't sound like nothing. What is it?"

"Oh, just . . . that bimbo who was hanging all over you that time."

I had some difficulty remembering whom she might be talking about. I finally did recall the tall blonde at the blackjack table, although I could no longer remember her name. "Is that still bothering you?"

"Not about her being in the restaurant with you that time, but . . ."

"What?"

"Yesterday."

"I wasn't here yesterday or I darn sure would have been with you, if that's what you're wondering."

She shook her head. "It's just that I heard her, well, asking about you. At the information desk."

"Is that all?"

"That seems quite enough to me."

"Look, I hardly know the woman. I don't even remember her name. I think there is a possibility that she has been asked to make up to me and keep an eye on me for business reasons. That's all it would be. And I don't happen to be interested, thank you." I gave her a kiss by way of guaranteeing the information.

"I thought you said you're a rancher."

"I am. I also make a few investments from time to time. There's a fellow out here who wants me to invest with him, but I haven't made up my mind if I will or not. That's all there is to it." I suppose I should have felt nine kinds of guilty for lying to Julie like that, but I didn't. It seemed kinder under the circumstances—and safer, too—to do that than to tell the literal truth. And if you wanted to stretch things far enough, that story could be pretty much true if carefully edited.

Julie sighed and nestled back down in the hollow of my arm. "I'm sorry, Carl. I don't have any right to be jealous of you anyway. I promised myself I wouldn't be, and that I wouldn't say a single word to you about it. It's none of my business what you do or with who. I'm sorry."

"I'll make a deal with you."

She looked skeptical. "What's that?"

"What is a deal? It's kind of an agreement wherein one party . . ." The dang girl struck me in the face. With a pillow. I pulled it off and grinned at her.

"Speak up, white man, or I'll use some Oriental tricks on you."

"You've *been* using Oriental tricks on me. I like them."

"Are you going to tell me what this deal is or not?" She picked up the pillow and menaced me with it.

"If you put it that way." I took the weapon away from

her, tucked it under her pretty head, and kissed her about as well as I knew how. I assume that was well enough because she didn't complain, and we almost got sidetracked into forgetting what we'd been talking about.

"The deal," I said when the breathing was more or less back to normal, "is that as long as I'm here, or for as long as you find it acceptable from your point of view, and anytime I'm within a hundred miles of Reno if you still want it so, Miss Julie, I hereby grant you full rights of jealousy, exclusivity, and the use of my knobby but willin' body. Okay?"

She squealed, and you'd have thought I'd just whipped out a pair of diamond earrings to gift her with. She jumped me with more energy than I thought she had any right to have left after what we'd just finished doing.

Darned if I didn't have some energy left too.

23

The dealers, the gamblers, the machines, and the tables were as unchangeable as granite. I might only have blinked my eyes instead of being away for days. Even the faces seemed unchanged. Certainly the ring and clatter of the slots was as before, and the bright interior lights coupled with dark glass at the distant doorways made it nearly impossible to tell day from night. Here, that seemed, in its own way, oddly appropriate.

Julie had gone to report in for work, and after a brief nap with the soft pleasure of her breath against my neck I was not ready to turn in for the night. I bought a roll of quarters and ambled through the rows of slot machines, lost those, and drifted to the blackjack tables.

The dealer was a blond girl in her late twenties or early thirties, cheerful and pleasant, helpfully instructing those who were new to the game, sympathizing or rejoicing as required with those who were not. My slim stack of house dollars rose slowly but nicely as the game progressed.

I drew a nine to a fourteen to go bust and watched while the dealer busted too. The luck of the draw. I really didn't mind. The man at my left had done the same thing, and he did seem to mind. He gathered up his five-buck tokens and moved to a different table.

"Are you still lucky for me?"

"Hmmm?"

It was the elegant-looking woman Julie said had been asking about me. I hadn't seen her slip into the just-vacated chair.

She smiled brightly. "I was wondering if you might be lucky for me again."

"I doubt it." I turned away from her and concentrated on the play, this time standing on eighteen and having the satisfaction of seeing the dealer quit at seventeen. Quite apart from the promise I had so recently made to Julie, I simply was not interested in the woman. After a couple plays she went away.

The pleasure of the game had gone with the woman, though, so after a few minutes I cashed in, coming out eight bucks ahead, which by casino standards must have been a great thing indeed.

Then I remembered the lost roll of quarters. They were still ahead of me. In the long run I guess they always would be. I found myself chuckling at my own flush of small pleasure to have been thinking myself ahead when I was not.

Which is no doubt the reason any casino loves to see a payoff to the patrons. It just brings them back for more.

I thought about going over to the sports bar with the big-screen cable TV hookup, but that was where Julie was working this evening. I didn't want to distract her from her work, so I headed instead for the cafeteria. Once I'd arrived and found Julie waiting for me, I hadn't gotten around to eating. Not that I regretted the delay, not by a long shot, but I was beginning to feel it.

I ate a leisurely meal and played a couple tickets of keno. The runner was a girl I had seen Julie chatting with several times before, but if she recognized me she gave no indication of it. She was pleasant but strictly businesslike.

On the way out of the restaurant I had company.

The long-haired hippy creep joined me.

"Coffee, Mr. Heller?"

"I was thinking about playing the slots again." Actually I had been thinking in terms of a hot shower and soft bed, but I sure didn't want to invite this craphead up to my room. It might only be a rented place to sleep, but for the moment it was my own personal, private place, and I didn't want his kind violating that privacy.

"If it's all the same to you, Mr. Heller, I don't much care for all the cameras in the casino."

I shrugged. Followed him back into the cafeteria and let him pay for two cups of coffee.

It had been, what, forty-five minutes at the most since the blonde had spotted me back at the hotel. They were an efficient crowd. It would have taken him nearly that long to drive in from the Red Hat. I certainly didn't think he would have been posted in town just waiting for me to get back. Littori didn't need my business that badly.

"I assume you have a reason for being here," I told him when we were settled at a table and he was spooning great mounds of sugar into his cup. "Or do you just enjoy my company?"

He was under orders. He didn't even scowl, though his eyes said there were a number of things he would have liked to do in response.

I looked across to the next table to make sure no one was paying attention to us. No one was, of course, but the family sitting there made me feel even harder toward my unwanted companion. They were a fortyish mom and pop in tourist outfits and a bright, fresh, innocent-looking teenage girl. The girl had a scrubbed look about her that emphasized her vulnerability and made me want to reach across the table and punch the creep in the mouth.

"Well?" I demanded.

He didn't answer right away. "You don't like me, do you?" he asked instead.

"Not worth a damn," I told him honestly enough. "I hope that isn't a requirement, because I don't think you like me a whole hell of a lot either."

"That isn't important."

"You're right. In both directions. Now what is it you're supposed to tell me?"

"Mr. Littori is out of town on business. Your business, as a matter of fact. He said if you got back before he did, I was to find you and tell you. Don't come around the place. We'll get in touch. It won't be but a day or two. Hang tight here. Okay?"

I nodded.

Across the room there was a security officer placidly munching a sandwich and having a glass of iced tea. He looked very much like a man taking a break, but I noticed that his eyes kept coming back to the hippy creep. If Littori's crowd was efficient, I thought, so was the security force here at the casino. Very forward-thinking folks. I began to worry about my reputation.

"You've delivered the message, now get out of here." I gave him a very obvious look of disgust and a wave of my hand to send him on his way.

The creep didn't like it, but then it hadn't been for his benefit. I just hoped the security man had seen it too.

"I haven't even finished my coffee."

"*Now*," I said with something of a snarl. This time the benefit was all his. He slopped coffee into his saucer getting the cup down and got the hell out in a scuttling hurry that seemed perfectly appropriate for his personality. I made it a point not to look toward the security guard after the creep was gone.

24

Listen, when an old boy from the Colorado high country tells you that a piece of scenery is spectacular . . . believe it.

Lake Tahoe is spectacular.

Rock-and-snow majesty of the Sierras rising practically straight up from the startling blue surface of the lake.

Incredible.

I couldn't believe my own stupidity. In all the times I had ripped into Reno in the past and spent my time behind the chutes at the rodeo arena, I had never once bothered to take the short drive up to Tahoe.

On the other hand, seeing it the first time with Julie in tow made those previous oversights forgivable.

I found a turnout from the highway that gave us an idyllic view of the lake and the touching-close mountains beyond it and parked the Beemer. Julie collected the tank bag with its thermos and box lunch she had somehow promoted from the hotel kitchens while I wandered off the right-of-way in search of a place to perch.

Below us, toward the lake, the slope was still drifted deep with crystallized snow from the past winter's falls, but up near the road there was a soft bed deep in needles from the massive trees—firs, I thought without being entirely certain—that thickly forested this country.

I found a sun-dappled opening far enough below the road that we could not be seen but was not soggy from melting snow, and we spread out for a picnic.

Not that my concentration was on the food. The girl was *much* more interesting.

We nibbled on the sandwiches for a while, nibbled on each other for a somewhat longer time, and eventually succumbed to the inevitable.

When we were once again buttoned and tucked and presentable, I lay back on the needles and lit a cigarette. Julie poured me the last of the coffee and propped my head up on her denim-covered thigh.

"Thanks." The coffee was only adequately warm, but it was a treat in that time and place and I enjoyed it.

"Carl."

"Hmmm?"

"Could I ask you something?"

"Sure." I closed my eyes against the brightness of the sun. Its heat made the miniature glade cozily warm, although the air was decidedly chill up here in the shade.

"Why are you here?" Her fingers were a soft pleasure as she stroked my forehead and temple. The temptation to drift away into sleep was strong.

"Because you are a beautiful girl and this is a beautiful day and a beautiful place. Because I like you very, *very* much. Because the combination of you and the day and the place are a joy to remember and to treasure. Because right now I'm a very happy fellow." I opened my eyes and smiled up at her. "I think that covers it."

She did not look nearly as happy as I felt just then. I sat

up and squirmed around to face her. "You look serious all of a sudden. What is it?"

"I didn't mean why we're here at this very moment, Carl. I meant, well, why are you in Reno?"

I almost made the mistake of wisecracking that we were in Tahoe, but that wasn't the kind of answer she wanted or needed just then.

"Combined business and pleasure," I told her, "you being the pleasure, even though I hadn't expected to have the incredible good fortune to find you here."

She nodded, but I noticed that she did not look me in the eyes when she did it. She was examining her thumbnail.

I reached out and touched her wrist. "Why?"

She looked at me this time, but there was a hint of concealed anguish in her eyes. "I . . . like you very much, Carl. I trust you. I *thought* I knew you."

"I hope you do. And I hope you know what I think and feel about you too, Julie. You're a very special, very wonderful girl. I wouldn't ever want to do anything to hurt you. But right now I'm beginning to think maybe I have, somehow. Have I?"

She sighed. And looked away. "This morning, before I clocked out, a friend of mine in security came by to have a word with me."

"Yes?" I made it a question, but I was afraid that I knew all too well the substance if not the exact wording of what had been said.

"She said she knew I was . . . fond of you. She said that might not be a very smart thing for me to do."

Damn. I'd never once thought about putting this good and innocent girl's job in jeopardy, but maybe I had already.

I wanted, quite desperately, to tell her the whole ugly truth.

What it came down to, I didn't want Julie or her friend in the security department or anybody else, known or unknown, to think ill of a Colorado low roller called Heller. It was, basically, as simple as that. I wanted Julie in particular to think well of me. Anything less would bruise the tender interior patches we call an ego. I just plain wanted folks to think well of me.

But, dammit, I *couldn't* say anything that would justify my odd actions and associations when I wasn't with Julie.

I didn't for a moment think that Julie was any kind of plant. Hell, I trusted her as much as she wanted to like and trust me.

But with the best and truest intentions in the world, Julie could unknowingly blow the inroads I had made with Tony Littori. Fat Tony, Falcone's people had called him, although I didn't know where that nickname might have come from.

Once assured, Julie could in complete innocence say something to her friend in security, a simple assurance that all was well. And that friend could mention it to one of the other security people. And if Littori had friends among the cops, who was to say he didn't have ears in the casinos too.

It was a chance I just could not take, and if I had to quit seeing Julie to take the pressure off her, well, that would just have to be a price to be paid.

"I don't understand," was all I told her.

"My friend said you have some . . . unsavory . . . connections here."

"I don't know who she might mean. The only connection I have here is you, and you are about as 'savory' a person as I've ever met."

Julie acted like she did not really want to go any further but felt compelled to do so. Probably she had made up her mind beforehand to see this through to whatever end would come. "Last night," she said, "you met with a man called George Byers. He is on the hotel's undesirable list."

George Byers would have to be the name of the long-haired hippy creep, then. "Honey, I can tell you in all sincerity that until just now I have never heard the name George Byers. I'm supposed to have met with him?"

She nodded. "In the Stage Door. Last night while I was working."

I allowed a look of comprehension to flow across my face. It was a form of a lie and I hated to do it, but I did it regardless. "Oh," I said. "Would this Byers fellow be some kind of pimp?"

Julie bit her lip and nodded again.

"He never got around to giving his name. I damn sure never asked him for one. He approached me last night, said he wanted to talk to me, and bought me a cup of coffee. When he told me what he had in mind, which he was offering free, by the way, I told him to shove off." I gave her a phony sigh. "I think I told you, someone wants to get an inside track into my investment plans. When that blond broad didn't work out, this was probably his second shot at it." I took her by the arm and got her to look at me. This time I wasn't spinning lies to her.

"Listen, Julie, if I'm causing you any trouble, the kind that could lose you your job or *any* kind of trouble, I'll back away. I won't see you again. I will damn sure understand." I gripped her hand and gave it a squeeze. "I told you already, girl, I wouldn't want to do *any*thing to hurt you. Not in the tiniest way. Please know that."

A small tear of liquid crystal caught the sunlight at the corner of her eye and rolled down her cheek.

Julie turned and flung herself into my arms. "I know you wouldn't. I already told my friend that. I know you aren't the kind of person who could be mixed up with people like that. I *know* what kind of person you are."

She was crying a little and kissing my neck a lot, and her breath was hot and disturbing against my flesh.

"Maybe it would be better if I did leave you alone."

"No!" She held me tighter. "No, Carl. You made me a promise yesterday. Do you remember it?"

"Very well," I told her.

"Well, I'm holding you to it for every second that you're in Reno. Every second, Carl Heller."

I nodded. I also made another promise to her, but one I did not speak out loud. If ever I thought for one minute that my being with this girl would hurt her, in any way at all, I was going to bail out. Hurt feelings can heal with time. There are other kinds of hurts that can never be healed.

Julie stood and took me by the hand, pulling me to my feet. "Come on now." She sniffled and brushed her forearm across her eyes and wiped her cheeks. "You promised to take me to Harrah's. I'm holding you to that one, too."

We gathered up the leavings of our picnic and walked back up the slope to the BMW.

25

The more I thought about it, the less sure I was of what I ought to do now.

Al Falcone's desires were very clear: no cops, no official involvement.

But I was only minimally interested in any rules and regulations set down by Falcone and his kind. Their interest was strictly in the risks Littori posed to their own profits, and I can't get real excited about protecting the interests of people who are motivated only by greed.

I admit it. I'm an old-fashioned, moralistic, probably quite silly SOB. And it would have pleased the hell out of me to see Tony Littori and *all* his friends spread across the headlines of every newspaper in the state of Nevada and locked up until it was box time for each and every one of them. Without the assistance of some people carrying badges and clout, I just couldn't manage that.

I thought about it a great deal, and I kept remembering all the things I'd heard about Nevada's organized-crime task force. Everything I'd heard about that crowd was that they were sharp and they were straight arrow. The temptation was awfully strong to pick up the telephone and bring them into it.

The main thing stopping me, quite honestly, was the

thought that I had committed a highly illegal act myself when I paid Littori for the girl named Linda. I wasn't entirely sure that I wouldn't be sharing cell time with Littori if I took the official route to redress. That I could do without quite nicely, thank you.

I thought about it for the better part of the night, while Julie was busy keeping the keno players happy, and in the morning when she went home to refresh her clothing and girl things, I reached for the telephone.

The voice that answered was one I thought I recognized.

"I need to see Falcone," I told the guy on the other end of the line.

At the very least, I'd decided, I should talk it over with him. Give him and his crowd a chance to cover themselves before I peached to the fuzz. Or whatever it was I would eventually end up doing. I honestly hadn't decided yet.

"The man said that wouldn't be possible," the voice told me.

"The man damn well better make it possible," I insisted. "It is definitely in his interests to see me."

"You're being foolish, pal."

"It wouldn't be the first time. But I do think he will want to have a say in things before I go any further. Pal."

There was silence for a moment. Then the guy said, "I'll have to check this. Where are you calling from?"

"My room at the MGM."

"Yeah, okay. Even we can't get a line into that switchboard. I'll call you back." He didn't ask for the room number. Obviously there was no need for him to. The line went dead, and I lay back on the bed to wait and smoke.

I really expected a fairly long wait, but there wasn't one. The phone rang in less than three minutes.

"That you, buddy?" It was a different voice this time.

"Everybody has to be somebody," I told him. "Who were you expecting?"

"Yeah, it's you all right."

"As long as you're happy with the connection," I said.

"The man wants to meet you."

"Good."

"Right now."

"Now?"

"That's what the man said."

"All right."

"Not at the hotel. There's no way he wants to be seen with you, if you know what I mean."

"I agree." My having a chat with Al Falcone was not exactly the sort of thing that would inspire confidence in Mr. Littori and his crowd.

"The man thinks this should be your morning to do the downtown casinos, buddy."

"All right."

"You know the shuttle bus to the Cal-Neva?"

"I've seen it."

"Go down right now and take the next shuttle. Get off downtown and take a walk through the casinos. Take your time about it and make sure nobody's paying any attention to you. Can you do that?"

"Can a buck boff a doe?"

"What?"

"I can do it."

"Okay," he said. "When you're sure you're traveling alone, keep on hiking past the casino district. All the way out to the Circus Circus. You know the big sign with the clown on it?"

"Uh-huh."

"Stop right under it on the corner there. A cab will be cruising." He gave me the taxi number. "Get in and ask to be taken to the Badlands. You got that?"

"Sure." I repeated it back to him. The Badlands, I figured, would be a restaurant or a club or simply a code. Whatever, the directions were easy enough to follow.

"All right. Get on it right now or you'll miss the connection."

I sighed. "Okay." The more I thought about it, the more I thought this was coming up on cop time for Mr. Littori and friends. But I owed it to Falcone to let him know before I did it.

Besides, if anyone in Nevada should know who the truly straight cops were, that son of a bitch should be the one. If I worked it right, Falcone could probably help me make the safe connection I needed.

"I'm on my way," I said, and the phone went dead.

I grabbed my cigarettes and lighter, scribbled a quick note to Julie to tell her I wouldn't be gone long—although I really expected to get back to the room before she did—and headed for the elevators.

With any luck, I thought, Littori and company might be in jail before nightfall.

I went out to the shuttle stand, remembering that this was the same place I had been picked up by my long-haired hippy creep friend George Byers not so very long ago, and took the free bus downtown into the heart of the gaudy casino district. A little seedier down there but nothing compared with Vegas. Reno was still basically a family-welcomed gambling town.

I kept an eye on my backside and circulated through

Harrah's Reno and Harold's Club and the Horseshoe and a good many of the rest of them, each one decorated with brightly colored come-ons promising that they had the best play and the biggest payoffs in Nevada, smiling at the streetside shills and rejecting offers of free play and even free money if I would just come inside to try their machines. The people around me seemed to be having an awful lot of fun.

When I was satisfied that I was indeed traveling alone, I passed under the famous Reno arch proclaiming it the "biggest little city in the world" and walked on to the huge clown sign outside the Circus Circus. That sign promised free circus acts for the kids and a big payback on the dollar slots for mom 'n' pop.

I hadn't been standing on the streetcorner two minutes before a cab bearing the correct number pulled up beside me. I got in and delivered my message.

"You got it, buddy." The voice belonged to the man I had so recently been talking to on the telephone. He apparently saw the recognition in my expression and gave me a grin, but he didn't say anything. This whole crowd out here, I thought, was definitely shy of public statements.

The cab whisked off into the heavy traffic, peeled away from the congested area, and headed in a circuitous route more or less trending to the northeast.

"You can relax," the guy said. "This will take a little while."

"All right."

I left the driving to him, not particularly interested in the sights on the outskirts of the city, and was damn well unprepared when he pulled to a stop beside a bus-stop bench.

"What . . . ?"

My friendly cabby had produced a .38 Chief's Special or some reasonable facsimile thereof. The blank, ugly eye of the muzzle was staring at my forehead.

And the guy getting in beside me from the bus bench had a small automatic in his hand, .32 caliber or thereabouts. The second man was my old and dear friend George Byers, the long-haired hippy creep.

"Did I make an error, George?" I asked him.

The grin he gave me was answer enough.

26

"Let me make a guess," I said. Reno was behind us now, and we were driving at a nice and legal rate of speed out into the desert, more or less in the same area where Byers had brought me to meet with Littori and the van that night not so very long ago. I had the distinctly uncomfortable idea that this time I was going on a rather different kind of ride.

"You didn't have the telephone bugged. Not at the MGM," I said. "So somebody slipped in and put a tattletale in my room. Right?"

Byers grinned at me. "By now some son of a bitch is wondering why you ain't answering the phone," he said. "You damn near pulled it off, though. Mr. Littori is due in tonight with a fresh shipment of goods intended for you.

Ain't he gonna be surprised when he finds out what you were up to? But of course by then it'll all be taken care of." The grin became wider. "Won't it?"

I didn't bother to answer, not thinking he really wanted one, but the creepy bastard might be right at that.

Like a complete damn fool, thinking I was on my way to meet with people more or less on my side of things, I had left my Smith & Wesson in the Beemer's tank bag. And that now-useless piece of luggage was at the moment lying undisturbed—and unreachable—on the dresser back in my hotel room. I keep telling myself that someday I'm going to learn that the only place a handgun can do you any good is in your damn *hand*. But I'm a slow learner.

At least Julie was out of it. At least, no matter what happened to me at the end of this ride—and I had no illusions that it was going to be any kind of a pleasure trip— she was out of it. The note I had left her said nothing about where I was going or whom I was supposed to meet.

No help there, of course, but I wouldn't have wanted any if it meant placing her in danger. I'd had that sort of thing happen to me once before, when an innocent woman had had to pay for one of my mistakes, and if nothing else was going right today, at least I could know that I wasn't hurting Julie. That was something. Under the circumstances, it would have to be enough.

I watched the dry, dreary countryside roll past the cab window. No green river course, this; it was dry and lonesome and barren of such encouraging signs as power poles and road markings.

Not that it was anything like the sandy dunes or true desert farther south. The abrupt, choppy hills here were covered with patches of vaguely green bunchgrasses and taller, thicker clumps of sage and creosote and cactus. Still, it was hardly inviting. And not at all inhabited. If I expected some local rancher to come riding to the rescue in a dusty pickup truck with his bugles blowing and guidons flapping in the wind, well, I was going to be somewhat disappointed. Whatever Byers and friend wanted to do with me, they sure seemed to have privacy and a clear field of combat to do it on.

"Getting nervous?" Byers asked. He acted like he enjoyed being able to ask it. No doubt he did.

I smiled back at the son of a bitch. "No, but maybe you should be."

That smart-ass answer turned out to be not exactly the best thing I could have said.

"Stop the car, Tim. Right now."

The cab came to a dust-swirling halt in the middle of the empty lonesome, and the driver turned around with his .38 at the ready. "What's wrong?"

"This prick don't act right, Tim. It just could be that he's carrying a beeper or something."

Tim grunted. "That'd be easy enough to fix."

"I think we better." To me Byers said, "Get out." He emphasized the instruction with a jab of his gun into my ribs.

If old Georgie had been alone, that would have been a dandy opportunity for me to make him eat that piece of foreign steel. But he wasn't alone, and Tim was holding his short-barreled Smith as if he knew how to use it. I got out of the cab.

"Strip," Byers ordered.

I thought about a whole lot of responses I could have

made . . . if only this or if only that. There weren't any "if only's" I could appeal to at the moment. I stripped.

I started to hand the clothes back in to Byers but he shook his head. "I don't wanta examine your rags. Might miss somethin', you know. Just throw them down. We'll pick 'em up later and carry them to where it won't hurt if they're followed."

I rather hated to admit it, but it was a sensible thing to do from his point of view. Make sure I couldn't be tracked to wherever we were going, then come back and leave a false trail to someplace else. The fact that I had no such gadgetry concealed in my clothes had nothing to do with anything. They were not going to take any chances. I dropped my clothes into the dirt on top of my shoes and tried to ignore the uncomfortable truth that a naked man *feels* totally vulnerable. Psychologically that is an immensely powerful reduction of the spirit. I hoped Georgie and Tim did not happen to know that.

"Get back in," Byers said.

I made no attempt to cover myself or to ask if I could at least retain my Jockey shorts. I didn't want to give the bastards that much satisfaction. I just got back into the cab. The vinyl part of the seat cover was unpleasantly hot against my thighs. At least there was fabric beneath my even more tender bare butt. Small favors and all that.

"Home, James," I said.

"Gee, it's gonna be fun killing you," Byers said with a grin.

27

"Get out."

We were at least fifty miles from downtown Reno, several hours' worth of driving on the barely visible track Tim had been following for practically forever through the empty country. I hadn't seen a trace of a real road in an awfully long time.

A half-hour or so before we had passed some dim tracks in the dirt that might or might not have marked the place where I had met Littori's van that night. Not that I really cared at the moment. It was of academic interest only.

"Get out?" I asked. "Here?"

Byers looked very happy. "Right here."

I glanced up toward the sun. It was past mid-morning now, climbing toward noon. With no clothes to shield me from it, it would be uncomfortable.

On the other hand, I thought, I probably would not be uncomfortable for very long.

"You know," I said, "I really don't care if I cause you a lot of bother cleaning this cab out."

I was looking at Byers. It was his partner, Tim, who clopped me over the left ear with the butt of his revolver.

"I think if you don't mind I'd like to get out of the cab now."

"Good idea," Byers said.

Damn, that hurt. Rubbing it didn't make it feel a bit better, of course, but I felt compelled to do it anyway. I also got out of the car. Byers and Tim joined me in the sunshine and fresh air of the Great Outdoors.

I took a look around. I wasn't really expecting to find anyplace to run to, and it is just as well that I didn't. I would have been sorely disappointed.

I don't think there is a natural, God-made spot anywhere in this end of Nevada that would be flat enough to host a football field, but Tim had chosen to stop at a place where there was a dandy field of fire for several hundred yards up the surrounding slopes in any and every direction. There was no chance I was going to run out of the range of even those pipsqueak firearms they were carrying.

"Nice country, ain't it," Byers observed.

"Lovely." I could already feel the weight of the sun on my back and backside. For the first time I began to regret my cow-country habit of keeping the body clothed and covered at all times. A California beach bum would probably be in seventh heaven out here, think it was just dandy country for sunbathing. Me, I was miserable. I had my granddad's habit of exposing my limbs only to bathe or make love.

"What it is, *Mister* Heller," Byers said happily, "is that you've taken your very last ride. If you know what I mean."

"Oh, I think I . . . ." I launched myself at his throat with all the intention in the world of getting a good grip on it. With any luck at all, I could keep hanging on past all the shooting and at least take this particular son of a bitch with me.

I never made it that far.

Tim moved awfully well. He chopped me across the back of the neck and had me down in the dirt before I got a fingertip on George Byers's scrawny neck.

"Now, now, *Mister* Heller." Byers kicked me in the belly. Not very surprisingly, it hurt like hell. That seemed to please him, because he did it again.

This time I was ready for it. I got a good hold on his ankle and gave it my best yank. I took the kick, but I got a little bit back from it because Byers came down hard on his tailbone, hard enough to make him cry out, and his pistol went flying.

I had a clear choice between ruining George Byers's throat or making a dive for the fallen gun, and I went for the gun.

It was the wrong choice.

A gunshot boomed hollowly in the silence of the high desert, and a great gash appeared in the dirt just in front of my reaching hand.

I just kept insisting on forgetting about that damned, competent Tim.

"Real still now, Heller. Just lie real quiet there." Tim walked far around me, his .38 trained on my head every step of the way, and retrieved Byers's pistol. He brushed it off against his pantleg and tossed the gun to Byers, who was finally getting back onto his feet.

"The way we like to work this," Tim said, "in the unlikely event the body might be found, see, is that we like to leave it without bullet holes. It's up to you, of course, but we prefer it that way." He grinned. "An' this way the turkey always figures he's got a fighting chance to make it out alive. Not that anybody's ever done it yet, but you always got to figure you got a chance."

It was mildly interesting to discover that this was old business to them. I had to wonder just how many times they had done it before.

I got to my feet and watched Byers assess himself for damages, then move toward me a step. "The boss prefers us to leave no bullet holes," he said, "but bruises don't show when the body's dried, an' a little softening up kinda helps insure the results, you know? So that's kinda what we figure to do with you, *Mister* Heller. Then we'll just drive away an' let you work things out the way you please."

"You don't mind if I object, do you?"

"Please do."

Tim pocketed his .38 and reached into the taxi for a sawed-off piece of baseball bat, then Byers moved in with his fists balled.

This was not, I thought, going to be an experience to brag about.

28

I guess I should have considered myself damn lucky that they hadn't quite finished the job of killing me.

Funny thing. I didn't feel very lucky.

They had done their work, Tim with efficiency and Byers with pleasure, and then they had driven away. At the time, I was only marginally aware that they were leaving. I don't even know that I *cared* they were going.

Once they were gone, I let the gray fog finish its job of veiling my brain, and I guess I passed out for a while.

When I came around again, the thing that was bothering me more than any of the hurts and the bruises they had inflicted in their carefully calculated way was the damn sunburn. That hurt worse than anything the two of them had been able to do. And judging from the sun, I hadn't been out in it for more than a couple hours.

I sat up, slowly and with great, great care, and took stock.

As it was, I could have been a whole lot worse off. I was battered and beat up on, but they seemed to have broken no bones. Whether that was due to Littori's orders concerning any eventual find of the body or was just my plain dumb luck, I couldn't tell and couldn't care. The fact that it was so was enough for the moment.

It was a damn long way from the ground to a standing position, but I made it and stood swaying and wobbling until my head felt like it was going to stay attached to my shoulders for a little while longer. I was weak and I was dizzy, but I was alive.

Tim's grinning comment about the turkey always thinking he had a chance kept coming back to me. Well, by God, the son of a bitch was right. I *did* think I had a chance.

No, dammit, that wasn't quite right. I did not think I had a chance, I *knew* it. A *good* chance, for as long as I believed it.

I didn't have any clothes and I didn't have a whole lot of strength. But by damn I had a whale of a lot of determination.

And, I told myself over and over, these ol' boys were used to dealing with a bunch of scared city types who'd flip out anytime they saw a piece of country without a roadside juke joint every hundred yards. Hell, I was used to country wilder than anything any of these crumbs could imagine.

Back home, I could put a leg over my old Belle mare and ride for two weeks at a stretch without having to look at another human being, and I'd done it time and time again.

I didn't happen to have a horse real handy here, and there wouldn't be any sweetwater mountain streams nearby. But all of that was only a matter of degree. I was still no stranger to lonesome country.

The first rule for survival anywhere is not to panic, but, hell, I wasn't thinking in those terms anyway.

The second is to take it easy and make it out in as much comfort as possible. Which, here, meant to get out of the sun while I finished doing some thinking.

I hadn't seen any trees worth noticing since we'd left Reno, but there were rocks aplenty, and wherever you find rock outcroppings you will find some of them that are overhung or water hollowed underneath or simply tall enough to afford some shade. My first order of business, then, was to go find myself a rock to crawl under.

Easier said than done. My belly and kidneys had taken enough punishment to make standing erect a painful experience, and the muscle pads on my thighs had taken even more while I was protecting my crotch from Byers's repeated kicks. Walking was not a delight. But it was possible.

Gimpy and limping, I hobbled back along the faint track where the car had driven.

Whoa, I told myself. I hadn't been paying all that much

attention, but as clearly as I could remember, we had not passed anything of interest for quite some time before we stopped.

So that might not be the best way to go.

For that matter, the route the car had come was the absolutely *most* logical way for a person to try to hike his way back to civilization.

And that route had been selected by Mr. Byers and the gentleman called Tim.

I wasn't about to make the mistake of thinking they had picked their spot at random. I knew—well, suspected— from personal experience that this was a road they had traveled more than once. Both because of my meeting with Littori that night and from the comments about other people being killed this very same way.

So I could logically assume that they had selected their put-out point with very great care.

They, of course, would fully expect their victims to try to hike back along the known route they had driven in on. It was psychologically almost imperative. The victim *knew* that civilization and good times were *right back in that direction*. If the guy could last until he got there he was home free.

Huh! As well organized and intent as this crowd was, I wouldn't be totally amazed if they posted Tim somewhere back along the route to keep an eye on it for a few days in the unlikely event that some poor sap could walk that far. If he did, he might well find himself in for another beating and a return to the starting point, do not pass Go, do not collect two hundred dollars, do not collect a drink of water.

The mere possibility that that could be so would be plenty

good enough reason for me to make my try in another direction. Any other direction.

And now was as good a time as any to alter course. Instead of trudging blindly back along the car tracks, I veered off to the side and passed around behind the nearest of the unending series of hills that made up this high-desert country.

Whether they had deliberately avoided letting me and their other victims see it or not I couldn't know, but on the other side of the hill that Tim had skirted driving in was a small and ugly rock outcropping in the soft desert soil. At the base of the thing was a niche just about big enough to cover a human body.

It covered mine, and nicely. The shaded stone felt quite chill against my sun-heated flesh, and I burrowed happily into the crumbling soil and dried vegetable litter beneath it until I was about as comfortable as a fellow could be. Under the circumstances, anyhow.

I blinked out into the glare of the sunshine, grinned, and closed my eyes for a nap. There would be time enough later to work out the details of what should be done next. For the moment, I could afford to rest and gather strength. And think about the pleasurable things that would take place— like with George and Tim and Fat Tony—when I got back to the real world.

When, dammit. When I got back.

29

I went cold, suddenly and totally icy. I'd been drowsing, about half-awake, watching the last of the shadows deepen into early night.

Now I could feel something moving behind me.

I knew what it was without turning to look. I could feel what it was, and I was afraid to move, petrified into complete immobility, with my heart beating madly and a sudden chill rattling my frame.

There, sliding dry and smooth against my unprotected skin, was a damned snake.

It came out of the rocks somewhere behind me and slithered alongside my bare butt, searched for a way over my leg with a gruesomely ticklish investigation, encountered my other leg, and continued on toward my feet with agonizing slowness.

I knew without looking that the damn thing was a rattlesnake. At least I was totally convinced that it was, if only because that was the worst possible thing I could imagine it to be. I do not *like* snakes. Up at the altitudes where I live and choose to play, I don't have to deal with them or think about them or be concerned about blundering into them. Up there, snakes of any type are next to nonexistent. Here in this lousy, high-desert country things seemed not to be the same.

It was logical enough, and if I'd been thinking about it I guess I would have expected something like this. But I had been thinking about the problems of getting out of here afoot. Justifiable, I think, but in hindsight a matter of poor judgment nonetheless. This snake and maybe ten thousand others just like it had been hiding from the heat of the sun. Now they would be crawling out of their dens in search of food and sun-warmed rocks to curl against. Jesus!

I thought about killing the thing. It was right down there behind my left calf. And that's the way they always do it in film and fable. Just pick up a rock and bash the thing before it can strike.

You bet.

I looked around. There were fist-sized rocks aplenty for me to choose from. Any one of them would have made pudding of a rattler's fragile skull.

I looked at them, assessed their size and heft, and left them the hell alone. I wasn't about to make *any* kind of motion that might irritate the snake.

At least there was no buzz of vibrating rattles. That was supposed to be encouraging, I thought. Or will they strike without rattling? I couldn't remember any of the many things I must have heard in the course of a lifetime, and certainly my own experience with them had been so limited as to be practically nonexistent.

Chill sweat had collected on my face and chest, and I could feel it running from my shoulders and down my back. That tickled, too, and the incongruity of being tickled in the midst of terror was almost too much to bear.

The body of the snake, not at all slimy or moist but dusty

dry and smooth, touched lightly against the sole of my foot. It was all I could do to keep from crying out and throwing myself aside.

Shit! I *couldn't* keep from it.

I yelped aloud and threw myself as violently and as far away from that nest of overhanging rock as a single, convulsive leap of cramped muscles could accomplish.

I landed hard enough to send the breath from my lungs in a whoosh that seemed extraordinarily loud in the complete stillness that surrounded me, rolled over, and scrambled upright, aware that I had left some skin behind. I did not particularly care about that.

Several feet to the rear I could hear now an alert buzz of warning, and in the faint remnants of the past day's light I could see a dark form that I might have mistaken for an aging cowplop if it had not been rattling.

I scuttled backward, completely unmindful of the pain from battered, abused, and now too-long rested and stiffened muscles.

Fair warning, you little son of a bitch, I told myself and the snake too. With no daylight, I was going to have to become cautious in ways that my normal experiences had not prepared me for.

I hobbled a few feet off, keeping an eye on the now-silent shadow that I *knew* was a snake and watching frantically for more shadows that *might* be snakes.

Relief and the cool night air on my drying sweat made me shake and shiver with a feverish chill. I would have gotten down on the ground to roll and coat myself with dust to dry and warm myself, but I did not want to expose any more of my body than was necessary to the lurking threat of snakes. There were, I figured, a whole hell of a lot more snakes

populating this area than I had seen. I was convinced of
that.

I moved away from there with a crablike, old man's gait,
bent over to minimize the discomfort of the pounding I had
taken, and climbed slowly uphill—in that part of Nevada
you are *always* either on a hill or beside one—until I could
locate the North Star. I have a good sense of direction, but I
wanted to take no chances of becoming lost here. Blind
faith in the infallibility of one's sense of direction could be
wrong only once out here. Then it might well be too late.

As it happened, the star was just about where I expected
it to be. For the first time since that rattler had routed me out
of my hidey-hole I began to stand and to breathe easier.

Reno was right back in that direction, toward the
southwest. From where I stood I could not see the bright
city lights directly, but the sky glow above the town was as
clear as those of Denver and Colorado Springs on the clear
nights back home.

After so much time to think about it, though, I was not
even tempted to walk toward that glow.

I had had ample time to think about and try to remember
the few times I had bothered to look at a map of the Reno
area.

Highways and even county roads were few out here, as
best I could recall, but over on this side of the state there
seemed to be more running north–south than east–west.

And I was not about to play Littori's game by following
the path he and his thoughtful boys had laid out for me. It
would be long and dry in that direction for sure, and I was
still at least seventy-five percent convinced that somewhere
along that backtrail at least one of the boys would be

waiting to make sure I could not make it out of the desert alive. I really wanted to disappoint them about that.

I got my bearings and faced east instead, away from the known but far-distant presence of civilization and comfort. I began to walk, *very* conscious of the presence of rattle-snakes in this miserable country.

30

Count all the small blessings, Carl, I told myself. The ground, for instance. Walking barefoot at home over the rock and hard gravel, my feet would have looked like ground round by now, and I'd have been leaving a bloody trail for miles behind me. But here the soil was loose and curiously soft, very easy to walk on except for the occasional encounter with prickly vegetation. I had very quickly learned to avoid stepping on anything but the dry bunchgrasses that grew here. The faint light from stars and half-moon were enough to permit me that measure of relief.

And, as I walked, my muscles loosened and warmed so that I was able to move easier, with much less pain than when I had started.

All in all, it was not really as bad as I had been afraid it might be.

Not that it was exactly a joyous romp in the great out-of-doors. Kind of like quarterbacking a pro football team—much, *much* easier done from the stands than the field.

Still, it could have been worse. I would rather do this than, say, make a solo climb of an ice wall. Which some fools I have met do for their winter relaxation. Although all in all I would have preferred being in Philadelphia.

I sighed, quit pretending I was only taking a breather when in fact I had been dangerously close to laying off for the rest of the night—it was only two or three, I thought—and marched on.

Somewhere up ahead I thought I could hear the growl of a straining engine.

Even thought I could hear the thing change gears.

Great imagination, Carl.

Less than an hour later, my sore but unbloodied feet touched the hard, dang-near-smooth surface of a dirt road carved into all this nothingness.

You want to know relief and pleasure and the leap-into-the-air kind of joy? Try that sometime. Try finding a road and hence a promise of civilization when such luxuries are supposed to be unavailable. Oh, I was grinning and walking with a free-swinging arm now. I turned south and followed the road at a glad clip.

It was not quite yet daylight when a barking dog told me I was back to the real world.

For the first time since dusk I became aware that I was naked. I found the twin-tracked path leading away from the road and hoped it would be a man and not a woman whom I roused from bed here.

No man. No woman either. The dog was shut up inside a house trailer—excuse me, mobile home—that sat as lonely and forlorn as an abandoned junk car in the middle of the emptiness here.

I could not even begin to guess at the reason a person would choose this place to make his home. A rancher? Possibly, although I saw neither fences nor pens to make that a likelihood.

A contrary, stubborn, independent recluse was just as likely. Someone choosing to go his or her own way, barely close enough to others to be able to find work of some sort, and that only when absolutely necessary.

We have some of that breed in the high country, people who reject the security of regular hours and the obligations of electric hookups and opt instead for a meager but free existence on their own terms. I saw no reason why Colorado might be blessed with all of that breed and Nevada given none.

And a blessing they are, too. Those I have met, and they have been many, have been good folks indeed. I like them. I think my grandfather and, perhaps even more, his father, who first homesteaded our land, would have felt perfectly at home in their company.

They are fewer now than they might have been at an earlier time in the westering of our country, but they are still around.

Judging from the bleakness of this modern-day homestead, I had probably found another.

Unfortunately, this particular reclusive homesteader was not at home at the moment.

The dog's barking would have awakened a deaf man, but I spent some time bashing on the aluminum door of the trailer anyway, with no greater results than the dog had gotten.

At least, I thought, I did not have to suffer the embarrassment of showing up naked at a stranger's door and asking succor.

It was coming dawn now, the light gathering, but the cold of the night was of concern now that I was no longer warming myself with movement.

I thought about breaking into the trailer, but I could not see the size of the dog, only hear its voice. It sounded bigger and nastier than I really wanted to tackle without a weapon or at least a boot to defend myself with.

Dropped helterskelter around the trailer were several sheds and disintegrating shelters, one of them obviously a privy, indicating that whoever this homesteader was, he was doing without running water. I decided to investigate the sheds before I broke into the man's home. Whoever and whatever he was—and he could have been the meanest SOB in the state—I was feeling positively benign toward him— or her—and did not want to do anything that would be abusive.

I used the outhouse and by the freshening light found a hand-pump well—you don't see a lot of those anymore— and treated myself to a long drink and a bit of a wash.

Lack of water had been one of my worries when Byers and Tim dumped me out of the cab, but oddly it had not been a problem. I wouldn't go so far as to say that dehydration is an underrated problem in the desert, but for damn sure a man can go overnight without having to wet his beak. My discomforts really had not involved water in the slightest, and I have to wonder if worry about it, like panic, is of greater danger than the fact.

At any rate, I filled up, drinking deeper than usual on general principles, and began poking around in the sheds.

Whoever this homesteader was, he was mechanically inclined if not particularly neat about it. There were hand tools scattered everywhere including on the ground, and beside the shed housing most of the tools was a rusting hulk that used to be a 1940s-vintage Packard. I complimented the fellow on his good taste.

In another shed were some chains and hoists and other junk I did not recognize and an elderly but reasonably clean Cushman motor scooter. I don't believe I had seen one of those since I was a kid.

I found some shop rags and the remains of an ancient beach towel, and the by now broad daylight of morning prompted me to fashion those into a cape and loincloth sort of covering.

Listen, the next time you see some movie with the natives running around next to naked, take pity on the poor slobs who were conned into doing the work. I will guarantee you they weren't comfortable doing it. At least my unprofessional arrangement of cloth was coming loose more than it was staying put, and when it was in place it was damn well uncomfortable.

Better than nothing, though. I was covered. I also looked around, but there were no trees I could play Tarzan in, so I set to thinking about how to get out of here.

There were no telephone or power poles leading to the place, so I didn't have to think about bothering the dog on that account.

I poked around the sheds some more and kept coming back to that motor scooter. A scooter, after all, is only a smaller relative of a motorcycle, and I am certainly comfortable with any kind of bike ever built. On an impulse I straddled the thing, twitched the choke, and kicked it over.

It caught on the third stroke. It sounded very much like my grandmother's dimly remembered gasoline washing machine from Sears. But it ran.

Shee-oot, I thought. I turned it off and checked the gas. The bent and pockmarked tank was full. The tires had a fair amount of air in them. The chain was intact, at least for the moment.

Hell, I thought, why wait around for my unknown host to return—which could take several days if he was not a dog lover—when I already had transportation available. Apologies and reparations could always be made later.

Shee-oot. Why not? I dragged the Cushman out of its nesting place and fired it up again, taking an extra moment to adjust my greasy loincloth to eliminate the high spots between seat and rump.

I had a startled moment of alarm when I automatically reached for the clutch and found none, then remembered that it was a piddling centrifugal-clutch arrangement and put the little bugger in gear. Everything seemed to be as it should be after all.

The only question now was which way to go.

31

When you get right down to it, at base there are only two ways an animal, human or otherwise, can react to confrontation: fight or flight. And nearly any animal, human or otherwise, will naturally prefer flight whenever possible.

Unless it is cornered, your average animal will run away from trouble. A bull elk could tear up any party of hikers in the woods, but instead they'll sidle away so quietly that most hikers will never know they've been close to elk. Any bear in the hills could rip up any party of people and their horses to boot, but you have to surprise them even to get a look at them. Even a mountain-lion tom will run from a perfumed poodle if it has the chance.

And probably people would get along better if we learned to run whenever we have the chance too.

But I've never been all that bright. Particularly when I'm mad.

Now that I was out of danger, full of water, almost clothed again, and had a way to get back to the hotel and safety, I was getting damn well mad.

Those sons of bitches had tried to kill me. I did not appreciate this.

They still thought they had killed me or were in the process of doing it. I wanted to inform them to the contrary.

Mainly, they had gone and gotten me pissed.

So instead of doing the sane, sensible thing and heading the two-wheeled relic south toward the highway and civilization, I turned it north, back the way I had come.

I kept having visions of Byers and Tim sitting in air-conditioned comfort, waiting for me to come staggering along their tracks so they could thump on me some more and take me back to dump me once again in the arid emptiness of this country.

Hell, if they *really* wanted another crack at me, maybe I should give them one.

Maybe I shouldn't, really.

But I was going to.

The elderly Cushman chugged and clattered back the way I had so recently walked, and I sat there getting madder and madder the more I thought about it. I have, I admit it, a highly developed capacity for indignation. It was working overtime now.

32

The catch vehicle was parked in the lee of a particularly abrupt hill about a quarter of mile off the path they would be watching, well within binocular view for someone waiting for a naked and thirsty man afoot. It was a Jeep of some CJ version with a roll cage, a bikini top for shade, and those bulbous, oversized tires that are such a handicap for mountain four-wheeling but that must really come into their own on the desert.

I suppose it could have been a teenage couple groping each other out here in the empty, but I really didn't believe that. Not in the noontime heat.

I should have arrived earlier and could have if I'd been sure of where I was going, but my sense of direction is only good. It ain't perfect. I had managed to find my way eventually, though, and since then had been paralleling the cab's track from a distance of about a mile, with frequent interruptions to work out where I was supposed to be.

The Cushman was an underpowered pup, had been way back when it was brand new and healthy, but the wide, soft tires had carried it well enough over the terrain I'd had to cross, and by now I was fairly well rested in addition to being spitting mad.

As soon as I spotted the waiting Jeep I cut the engine and propped the scooter against a rock. The kickstand, assuming it had ever had one, was no longer attached.

"Howdy, fellas," I whispered. I think I was grinning then, and I would not swear that my ears hadn't gotten pointy and that my teeth hadn't sharpened themselves. I was really wanting to lay hands on those old boys so I could do some snapping and snarling.

Damn, I wanted them.

It is probably an awfully good thing that I couldn't see myself, because I undoubtedly would have looked silly as hell if anybody'd been watching. Barefoot and bareheaded, wearing a loincloth made out of oil-soaked shop rags and a dirty terrycloth towel for a cape, no weapons except anger and a rock I had picked up along the way, I went hunting. Creeping and crouching and sneaking along.

Must have looked silly.

Still, the stalk was one any novice bowhunter could have made.

The guy in the Jeep—I could see soon enough that there was only one—was concentrating on the tire tracks, and I was coming up behind him.

I probably could have simply walked up on him in plain sight, but I wasn't willing to take that kind of gamble. Gambling is just fine for the casinos, a lot of fun even, but there is only money at stake there. Here I was gambling with something a whole lot more valuable, and whoever was in that Jeep quite certainly had a pistol handy and possibly a rifle as well.

Like I said, the stalk was no big deal, just a matter of time and caution, and eventually I was within ten yards or so of the Jeep, crouching behind the last cover available.

It was Tim who was waiting there, and I felt a pang of disappointment. I'd been hoping it would be George Byers, my long-haired hippy creep chum.

Later, I promised myself.

I examined the rock I had found, compared it with several others conveniently available, and decided to stay with what I had. It was fist sized and more or less rounded, with a slight projection on one side, which I held pointing outward. Small enough to be handled easily and heavy enough to do some damage. Just about right, I thought.

I got a good grip on the rock and bent low. When I moved out into the open and began ghosting up behind the Jeep, I was ready to make a jump for Tim if he should happen to turn my way.

Tim seemed to be—I damn sure hoped he was—
completely unaware of any possibility of danger.

He raised his binoculars, casually glassed the track out
ahead of him, then dropped the binoculars back onto the
passenger seat beside him.

He fumbled around for something down between the
seats and a moment later came up with an Igloo insulated
water jug. I was close enough to hear the muffled rattle of
ice inside it when Tim uncapped the spout and drank
directly from it. I made a face. It's an inconsiderate SOB
who drinks direct from the spout of a water jug.

But then, in fairness, Tim did not yet know that he was
going to have to share that jug.

I stood upright and catfooted up behind him with my rock
held at the ready.

Tim was partially protected by the tubular steel roll cage
on the Jeep, so I shifted the rock to my left hand, ready to
swing it in a broad sweep through the open space where a
door would have been if the CJ had been set up for weather
protection.

I moved on, very slowly and carefully now, until I was
close enough to touch him on the shoulder. He looked bored
and hot and sleepy.

"Hi."

The reaction was all a person could ever hope for.

The poor son of a bitch jumped so bad he almost came
tumbling out the side of the Jeep, and when he saw me
standing there smiling at him, his eyes popped wide and he
went fishbelly pale in half a heartbeat of time.

Tim's mouth sagged open, and his right hand twitched.

I don't really know if he was having the presence of mind
to reach for a gun, and I guess it really didn't matter.

As soon as I saw that flicker of motion, I swung my rock in a fast sidearm sweep that came whipping in under the canvas top of the Jeep and landed square over Tim's wide, panicked eyes.

I was still mad, and I hit him harder than I realized or intended. I could use the excuse that it is harder to judge if you are striking with the left hand and are right-handed, but I don't know that that had much to do with it.

Whatever, the bone collapsed under the impact, and Tim's face was turned from white to red.

He never made a sound. Just that quickly, the entity that had been Tim was no longer inhabiting that body.

The thing where Tim used to live spilled off the seat onto the ground with its legs twisted and caught under the steering wheel.

It lay there with an oozing red mush where its face used to be. The eyes, protruding and cocked outward, were a bit hard to look at.

I spun away and went loping off to the side to find a good place to throw up.

I was shaking and was covered with a quick rush of oily sweat that had nothing to do with the heat. My knees were not up to the job of supporting me, and I sank to the ground.

Eventually, I guess it wasn't more than a few minutes although it felt like longer, I was able to get up again and wobble away.

There was a chair-high rock nearby so I staggered over to it and sat down. Going back and sitting in the Jeep did not seem at all desirable just then.

I still had the dry heaves and bent over, retching.

My sight fastened on a pile of dry rubbish littering the ground here, and all of a sudden I was mad all over again.

And there was, by God, no longer a trace of remorse for that son of a bitch Tim or for any bastard like him.

Right there at my feet were the desiccated remains of what had once been two human beings.

At least two. There might have been a third. I couldn't really tell for sure, because a good many of the bones had been rearranged or dragged off by coyotes or whatever small scavengers and predators inhabited this inhospitable country.

But there were at least two. I could tell that from the pair of mummified skulls, with scraps of leathery, sun-cured skin and hair still attached, that stared back at me.

Most of the flesh was long since gone from the bodies, but the length of remaining hair and the presence on one of them of a tarnished, gold-washed necklace made me believe that both of them had been girls.

I sat there on that rock and stared at them for a long, long time. Grieving for these long-dead kids. Wishing I had been able to do something when it would have been possible to help them.

I shook my head. Probably I would never know who they had been or why they had been disposed of in this vulgarly savage fashion. Probably no one ever would. Even that shit Littori might have forgotten by now. They had been there for quite some time, judging by the appearance of things.

Why? I couldn't know. Too young. Too old. Too unwilling to accept the cruelties of the fate that had put them in Littori's hands.

There could have been a thousand reasons. Or none. Littori could simply have given his boys the pleasure of someone else's agony, and these unfortunates might have been the ones who were required to pay that price.

I sat looking at the tatters of dry, sunbleached hair attached to those mummified, faceless skulls and could not even be certain what color their hair had been.

I tried, desperately tried, to remember the length and color of hair in that photograph Walter had shown me of his runaway grandniece. I couldn't.

For all I knew, one of these kids could have been that child.

If it was, I hoped none of that good and kind man's family ever learned about it. Better to hope that she was rebellious and hateful but somewhere still alive than to be faced with a reality of this kind of ugliness.

Bastards, I thought. Any milk of human kindness that might have been in me was curdled now.

I said my apologies and my good-byes to the dead girls and walked with a steady and an eager step back to the Jeep.

Tim's body no longer bothered me. I hauled it out of the vehicle and stripped the clothes and shoes from it.

They were not a good fit and they were slightly soiled with blood, but they would do. I dressed in Tim's clothing, drank deep from the Igloo, shoved Tim's short-barreled .38 into my pocket, and crawled in behind the wheel of the Jeep.

Even if I dragged half the cops in Nevada back to this spot and explained it to them in detail, no prosecutor would ever have a chance at proving Mr. Anthony Littori remotely responsible for any of it.

If I'd ever harbored any thoughts about ringing in the duly constituted authorities, those notions were damn sure gone now.

I started the engine of the CJ and headed for Reno.

33

I felt no sense of hurry whatsoever. There was an inevitability about it that took away any sense of urgency.

I drove back to the MGM, got another key to my room from the desk, and changed into my own clothes. I had been mildly concerned that Julie might be in the room waiting for me, but there was only a note asking me to call her when I returned.

With my own Smith & Wesson M59 in the small of my back and Tim's revolver in my pocket, I hotwired the BMW—my keys were as unavailable as my wallet—and drove at a law-abiding pace south of town.

The girl, Linda, had been vague about the exact location of Littori's little hideaway for his "special" girls, but she had been precise about its description and almost certain about its direction from town. And I could take as much time as I needed to find it.

It was past dark before I did locate it. The girl had been sure of her description of the gate and driveway, curving back around one of the omnipresent Nevada hills with a no-trespassing sign posted beside a chain across the entrance.

There was no wall, though, only a ditch on either side of the chained driveway, and the Beemer was no respecter of barriers intended for automobiles. I rode into the ditch and up the other side and around the closure that tried to separate me from my old friend Tony.

The man was back in town with a fresh shipment of special goods, George Byers had said. Fine. That should mean he would be here watching over his merchandise.

I followed the driveway around the hillside to the big modular home Linda had told me to expect.

Security? She had given me a look of great disgust. Don't be an ass. No one had to be kept there under lock and key. They were all there because they *wanted* to be. Tony was *good* to them. He was finding them jobs. Setting them up. Giving them freedom from the unwanted drag of whatever home or family they had run from. Come off it, man. He didn't need no locks on the place.

I was grinning again.

Mister Littori did not need locks to keep them in and did not want any of them to think he might. The Red Hat was a regular fortress, but this place was wide, wide open.

I mentally thanked him for being so considerate.

I parked the bike on its not particularly trustworthy sidestand and left the engine ticking over.

No one seemed to have been watching for my approach. I wouldn't have cared if anyone had been.

I felt tall and lean and hungry as I stalked up the flagstone walk to the front door. The hunger had nothing to do with food.

I tried the door without knocking; it opened to the turn of the knob.

From somewhere in the back of the place—it was bigger than I had expected—I could hear voices. High pitched, happy, girlish voices. Voices full of innocent delight. I followed the sound of the voices.

There was a floodlit patio behind the house. Beyond it, an aboveground swimming pool with sidewalls of blue-painted corrugated aluminum.

Tony and his merchandise were there. They were having a party.

I stopped in the doorway and took a moment to see.

There were nine girls ranging in age from a guessed thirteen or fourteen to probably no more than sixteen. At least five of them were smoking hand-rolled cigarettes, and on a glass-topped coffee table in the center of the group was an assortment of refreshments. Not your ordinary old crap like chips and dip, but a bowl of a leafy stuff that I assumed was marijuana along with smaller dishes holding pills of many colors and a white powder that I did not think was sugar. There were matches and cigarette papers and some short lengths of soda straws ready for convenient sniffing.

Lovely parties this fellow gave.

The genial host himself was reclining in a lounge chair on the right side of the patio, with his guests ranged around him on chairs and chaises, most of them wearing bathing suits, the others in shorts and tube or halter tops.

One of the girls—she couldn't have been more than fourteen, if she was that old—was curled kittenish on Tony's lap. She looked like a cute, ordinary kid, and he was fondling her slim, barely budding body with complete unconcern about the others looking on.

Not that any of them seemed to mind. They all seemed to be having a lovely time.

Beyond them, in the pool, were two others swimming and splashing. I could not see who they were because of the glare of the floods, but one of those in the pool was an adult male, the other a girl.

"The piper wants to be paid," I whispered to Tony Littori. "I came to act as his collector," I whispered a little louder.

I pulled out my Smith, flicked off the safety, and thumbed it back to full cock even though it's a double-action pistol. The trigger pull is much lighter if it is already cocked. The blue, cold steel felt good in my hand. I walked out onto the patio among the party-goers.

Littori's eyes popped wider than Tim's had done. If he thought he was seeing a specter, well, perhaps in a way he was. His own.

He shoved the girl off his lap and tried to come to his feet. The front of his slacks was wet.

Perhaps I could justify it by claiming that he was going for a gun. The plain truth is that I don't know whether he was or not. I didn't look. Didn't care. Still don't.

I leveled the Smith and pumped five rounds into the bastard's chest as fast as I could trigger them, and Anthony Littori was as dead as his boy Tim.

I was aware, as if from a distance, of cries and alarms and running bodies as the children scrambled away in terror.

In the pool, a man's head broke water and stared at me. It was, I saw with joy, George Byers, his long hair plastered to his head.

He dove beneath the ruffled, brightly lighted surface of the pool, and I mounted the steps to the slippery platform where the swimmers entered and left the playground.

Byers could not stay under but so long. His recent playmate had already left, vaulting over the far edge of the pool and disappearing into the night beyond it. I waited, able to see him clearly in the lights.

When he did come up, unable to hold his breath a

moment longer, I had no idea if he had become disoriented
or if he was attacking me, nearly as naked as I had been the
last time he saw me. Whatever the reason, he came up
directly toward me, lunging at me with hatred and fear
pulling his face into a contorted mask.

He came lurching out of the water at my feet, and thunder
rolled from the muzzle of the Smith for the second time.

When Byers fell back into the pool, he was quickly
engulfed in a spreading billow of dark maroon as the red of
his blood met the blue of the lighted water.

I pushed on the safety of the Smith and watched with
satisfaction as the disconnected hammer fell harmlessly and
safely into place. I put away the gun and turned to walk
back to the waiting BMW. There was no sign now of any of
the girls. I was sorry about that. I would have liked to
explain to them what they had escaped. But I was more glad
that they had escaped it than I was sorry that they did not
know the danger they had been in.

The night air felt clean as I remounted the Beemer. Quite
unlike the weight of the desert sun. It felt crisp and fresh
and very good, and breathing it was like taking a drink of
spring water running fresh and cold from the earth.

I drank of it and was glad to be alive.

34

I lay with a pair of thick pillows plumped behind me, a pot of room-service coffee and the remains of a huge, room-service breakfast on one side, Julie's warmth and gentleness nestling close on the other.

Room service had brought us a morning newspaper too. Julie was not particularly interested, but I several times read through the page-one story about a drug-related double slaying that had taken place south of Reno the night before.

There were, a police spokesman had told reporters, no witnesses to the killings, but evidence at the scene showed that a large quantity of drugs had been in use there before the murders. The killer or killers had stolen drugs from the patio of the suburban home, but a large stash was found locked in a wall safe during the investigation.

One of the girls obviously had had the presence of mind to sneak back and lift the goodies from the coffee table once I was gone.

Reading about it and the entirely plausible story the police had concocted, I could almost believe that it had happened that way.

Their version gave my memory a growing detachment, and since the memories were not something I particularly wanted to retain, I reread and welcomed the official line.

It would do quite as well as any, I thought, although perhaps the truth would have been better if it could have been discovered.

People—parents, kids, every-damn-body—needed to know that there were bastards and creeps like Anthony Littori and George Byers.

But it wasn't my place to tell them. I would have, but I couldn't do that without telling the police, too. And this was a situation, I decided, where what *they* did not know would not hurt *me*. Selfish? Maybe. But I expect I can live with that.

I yawned and felt Julie stirring contentedly beside me.

We were interrupted by the telephone.

"Carl?" I recognized the voice. It should have come from the mouth of a high-powered businessman, but instead it was only another creep, almost as rotten as Littori had been.

"Uh-huh."

"There's a package waiting for you down at the desk. Just like we agreed."

I thought, briefly, about all the responses I could have made. Indignant ones and holier-than-thou ones and nasty ones. I thought about them, but I didn't make them.

Thinking about them, being reminded about all the myriad reasons for them, I was really not a hundred percent certain that I was a lick better as a human being than this creep Al Falcone.

That, I realized, was something I was going to have to work out before too awfully long.

I looked at Julie, gentle and trusting at my side, and hoped as much as wondered that I might be good enough to be worthy of her company. I touched her cheek and ran a fingertip lightly across her breast and was given the immeasurable reward of a guileless, joyful smile.

"I'd rather not talk about it," I said into the telephone.

"No need to," Falcone said. "We're square now."

"Good-bye." I hung up.

"Who was that?" Julie asked.

"The man about the investments," I lied easily.

"Are you going to invest with him?"

I shook my head. "I don't think I want any more business in Reno. Just pleasure."

"Does that mean you have to go home?"

"Not for a while," I said. "Not until you're ready for me to."

"That could be a long time," she said with a sweet smile.

I folded her into my arms and buried my face in the clean scent of her hair and realized that I had begun to tremble.

My throat ached from wanting to tell her the truth. That I would not be leaving immediately. That I would not be leaving at all until her gentleness had healed the hurts within me and I could leave as a whole man again, with the ugliness of inhumanity buried and left behind here in Reno.

I hoped that when that did happen I could leave it here, that it would stay buried and perhaps someday even forgotten.

I ached to tell her that and more, but I did not dare try.

Julie raised her face and kissed me, and I held her very close.

She was kind enough and sensitive enough and knowing enough not to ask me why I was crying.

ABOUT FRANK RODERUS

Like so many of my generation, and just like the song says, "my heroes have always been cowboys." I have a deep and abiding love for the American West, what it taught us, and what it stands for. But not until I moved into the high country, far from grocery stores and modern services, did I realize how very much alive the spirit of the West truly is.

Carl Heller is a product of imagination. But he could as easily be friend and neighbor.

Here where addresses are given in terms of direction from ranches and valleys, creeks and mountain peaks, the people are independent of spirit and free to rise or fall on the basis of the strengths God has granted them. Carl Heller is, quite simply, one of them.

The situations he finds himself in are taken from the newspaper headlines of today and of tomorrow. They are a part of the daily fabric of the modern West. Some of them have already happened; all of them could happen.

And like any good friend, Carl and I share many interests, many loves. We both appreciate the feel of a strong-running motorcycle swooping the curves of Ute Pass or Florissant Canyon. We both are enamored of the American Quarter Horse with its great heart and quick feet. We both dote on the brisk, clean air and the magnificent vistas of the West. In one respect I have been more fortunate than Carl, because I have a family with whom I can share these pleasures. Carl, though, is basically a friend and neighbor with whom I would be glad to share my hunting camp.

THE COYOTE CROSSING

by Frank Roderus

Sneaking across the border wasn't just illegal—for Heller it could be downright lethal. To help a pain-wracked former lover fulfill a final promise, Heller agrees to go undercover south of the border to investigate the disappearance of a young Mexican last seen trying to buy his way into Texas. Heller is quickly caught up in a dangerous cross fire as he cozies up to the local "coyote"—that slimy breed of creature who takes desperate Mexicans across the border in the dead of night for a heavy fee and then, more often than not, sets them up to be robbed, beaten, even raped by bandidos. The frightened prey are powerless, they cannot turn to the authorities—and even if they could, nobody seems to care if a few less wetbacks make it to the other side. Nobody, that is, except Heller . . . and that ol' mountain boy knows more than one way to skin a coyote.

Look for THE COYOTE CROSSING, the next Carl Heller adventure, on sale April 1, 1985, wherever Bantam Books are sold.

WHODUNIT?

Bantam did! By bringing you these masterful tales of murder, suspense and mystery!

☐	24595	**THE TURN OUT MAN** by Frank Roderus	$2.95
☐	24499	**THE VIDEO VANDAL** by Frank Roderus	$2.95
☐	23117	**RAIN RUSTLERS** by Frank Roderus	$2.95
☐	24285	**SHE CAME BACK** by Patricia Wentworth	$2.50
☐	25008	**MIND OVER MURDER** by William Kienzle	$3.50
☐	24288	**DEATH IN FIVE BOXES** by Carter Dickson	$2.50
☐	24035	**THE DEATH ADVERSARY** by Agatha Christie	$2.95
☐	25084	**ROSARY MURDERS** by William Kienzle	$3.50

Prices and availability subject to change without notice.

Buy them at your local bookstore or use this handy coupon for ordering:

SPECIAL
MONEY SAVING
OFFER

Now you can have an up-to-date listing of Bantam's hundreds of titles plus take advantage of our unique and exciting bonus book offer. A special offer which gives you the opportunity to purchase a Bantam book for only 50¢. Here's how!

By ordering any five books at the regular price per order, you can also choose any other single book listed (up to a $4.95 value) for just 50¢. Some restrictions do apply, but for further details why not send for Bantam's listing of titles today!

Just send us your name and address plus 50¢ to defray the postage and handling costs.

THE THRILLING AND MASTERFUL NOVELS OF ROSS MACDONALD

Winner of the Mystery Writers of America Grand Master Award, Ross Macdonald is acknowledged around the world as one of the greatest mystery writers of our time. *The New York Times* has called his books featuring private investigator Lew Archer "the finest series of detective novels ever written by an American."

Now, Bantam Books is reissuing Macdonald's finest work in handsome new paperback editions. Look for these books (a new title will be published every month) wherever paperbacks are sold or use the handy coupon below for ordering:

- [ ] SLEEPING BEAUTY (24593 * $2.95)
- [ ] THE MOVING TARGET (24546 * $2.95)
- [ ] THE GOODBYE LOOK (24192 * $2.95)
- [ ] THE FAR SIDE OF THE DOLLAR (24123 * $2.95)
- [ ] THE ZEBRA-STRIPED HEARSE (23996 * $2.95)
- [ ] MEET ME AT THE MORGUE (24033 * $2.95)
- [ ] THE IVORY GRIN (23804 * $2.95)
- [ ] THE WAY SOME PEOPLE DIE (23722 * $2.95)
- [ ] THE CHILL (24282 * $2.75)
- [ ] THE GALTON CASE (22621 * $2.75)
- [ ] BLACK MONEY (23498 * $2.95)
- [ ] THE DOOMSTERS (23592 * $2.95)
- [ ] THE NAME IS ARCHER (23650 * $2.95)
- [ ] THE BLUE HAMMER (24497 * $2.95)
- [ ] FIND A VICTIM (24374 * $2.95)

Prices and availability subject to change without notice.